TIRRA LIRRA BY THE RIVER

JESSICA ANDERSON (1916–2010), née Queale, was born in Brisbane, the youngest of four children. Her mother was a part of the Queensland Labour Movement, and her father, a former farmer, worked in Brisbane teaching farmers how to treat disease in stock and crops. As a child she was mocked by her schoolmates for a speech impediment, and she left school at sixteen upon the death of her father. At eighteen, she moved to Sydney and labored at various odd jobs, including working in factories and designing electric signs; it was a time in her life she later characterized as "very poor but very free." She eventually met Ross McGill, a painter, and they moved together to London. There, Anderson worked as a typist and magazine researcher. She later claimed to have written articles, as well, under numerous pen names, but she remained highly secretive about those publications. After marrying McGill in 1940, she returned with him to Sydney, where she worked as a fruit picker in the Australian Women's Land Army. They had a child together—Laura—but she divorced McGill in 1955 and married Leonard Anderson, whose wealth permitted her to quit working and spend more time writing. Her first novel, *An Ordinary Lunacy*, was published in 1968, when she was forty-seven, to rave reviews. She would subsequently go on to capture numerous prizes for her work, including twice winning Australia's most prestigious literary prize, the Miles Franklin Award: in 1978 for *Tirra Lirra by the River*, and in 1981 for *The Impersonators*. Anderson died in Sydney at the age of ninety-three.

ANNA FUNDER is one of Australia's most acclaimed and awarded writers. In 2012, her novel *All That I Am* won Australia's most prestigious literary award, the Miles Franklin Prize, along with seven other literary prizes. Funder's nonfiction book *Stasiland*, hailed as "a classic," won the 2004 Samuel Johnson Prize. Both books have been international bestsellers and are published in twenty countries. Funder lives with her husband and three children in New

THE NEVERSINK LIBRARY

I was by no means the only reader of books on board the Neversink. Several other sailors were diligent readers, though their studies did not lie in the way of belles-lettres. Their favourite authors were such as you may find at the book-stalls around Fulton Market; they were slightly physiological in their nature. My book experiences on board of the frigate proved an example of a fact which every book-lover must have experienced before me, namely, that though public libraries have an imposing air, and doubtless contain invaluable volumes, yet, somehow, the books that prove most agreeable, grateful, and companionable, are those we pick up by chance here and there; those which seem put into our hands by Providence; those which pretend to little, but abound in much. —HERMAN MELVILLE, *WHITE JACKET*

PRAISE FOR JESSICA ANDERSON
AND *TIRRA LIRRA BY THE RIVER*

"Finely honed structurally and tightly textured, [*Tirra Lirra by the River* is] a wry, romantic story that should make Anderson's American reputation and create a demand for her other work."

—*THE WASHINGTON POST*

"In Jessica Anderson's ... acclaimed novel *Tirra Lirra by the River*, a single, singular voice brilliantly narrated the story of a woman's escape from an intolerable life—instant gratification for the reader."

—*THE NEW YORK TIMES*

"There may be a better novel than *Tirra Lirra by the River* this year, but I doubt it." —*THE PLAIN DEALER* (CLEVELAND)

"Anderson writes some of the best English in the language right now, and any mode she turns to is of interest ... [*Taking Shelter* is] a beguiling juggling-act of attitudes, new realities, and faultless style."

—*KIRKUS REVIEWS*

"Su   *rra*
b

A L

1/15

"Through Miss Anderson's artistry, her gifts for observation, insight and humor, each character comes to life and proves essential to the complex story . . . The characters in *The Only Daughter* are often startled by their own behavior, delighting or distressing one another and themselves. For the reader, there's the satisfaction of their 'roundness,' as defined by E. M. Forster—they're very 'capable of surprising in a convincing way.'" —*THE NEW YORK TIMES*

"Anderson conveys this heartwarming story [*Taking Shelter*] in an oblique but witty style, scattering insights and surprises throughout." —*PUBLISHERS WEEKLY*

"[*The Only Daughter*] is an exquisite novel of unforced volume and graceful, easy tempo . . . Anderson's great care in judging none of the characters makes them all vivid and completely believable . . . The arc of the novel is never stiff, always pliable, moving shrewdly back and forth between comic realism and social analysis. A strong, loose-jointed family novel altogether—totally convincing in its canny ear for the rhythms and tones of domestic alliance/warfare." —*KIRKUS REVIEWS*

TIRRA LIRRA BY THE RIVER

JESSICA ANDERSON

AFTERWORD BY ANNA FUNDER

MELVILLE HOUSE PUBLISHING
BROOKLYN · LONDON

TIRRA LIRRA BY THE RIVER

Originally published by Macmillan Company of Australia Pty Ltd, 1978
Copyright © 1978 by Jessica Anderson
Afterword copyright © 2014 by Anna Funder

First Melville House printing: October 2014

Grateful acknowledgment is made to the Mitchell Library,
the State Library of NSW, in Sydney, Australia, and to
librarian Richard Neville, for his assistance with this edition.

Melville House Publishing   8 Blackstock Mews
         145 Plymouth Street   and   Islington
         Brooklyn, NY 11201   London N4 2BT

mhpbooks.com facebook.com/mhpbooks @melvillehouse

Library of Congress
Cataloging-in-Publication Data

Anderson, Jessica, 1916–2010.
  Tirra Lirra by the river : a novel / by Jessica Anderson.
    pages   cm
  ISBN: 978-1-61219-388-5 (pbk.)
  ISBN: 978-1-61219-389-2 (ebook)
  1. Women—Australia—Sydney (N.S.W.)—Fiction.   I. Title.

PR9619.3.A57T5 2014
823'.914—dc23

                                        2014002830

Design by Christopher King

Printed in the United States of America
1 3 5 7 9 10 8 6 4 2

The characters in this story are imaginative constructions.
Only the houses on the point are taken from life.

TIRRA LIRRA BY THE RIVER

I ARRIVE AT THE HOUSE WEARING A SUIT— greyish, it doesn't matter. It is wool because even in these subtropical places spring afternoons can be cold. I am wearing a plain felt hat with a brim, and my bi-focal spectacles with the chain attached. I am not wearing the gloves Fred gave me because I have left them behind in the car, but I don't know that yet.

The front stairs are just as I visualized them on the plane, fourteen planks spanning air, like a broad ladder propped against the verandah. The man who drove me here from the railway station sorts his keys as he bustles to take precedence of me. He is about sixty, tall and ponderous, with a turtle head. He introduced himself on the railway platform, but already I have forgotten his name. I am exhausted, holding myself by will-power above a black area of total collapse. My nephew in Sydney warned me about the train journey. 'Six hundred miles, Aunt Nora,' he said. But I wouldn't listen; I said I simply adored trains. 'You won't adore that one,' said Peter. But I said of course I should; I adored all trains.

The truth is, I was terrified to fly again.

As I follow the man across the verandah I hear my own footsteps, like a small calf on a quaking bridge, and think of the last time I crossed it, on my confident high heels, to trip down those stairs to the taxi. Mother and Grace standing here, and myself running down the path to the yellow taxi, which waits where the man's car stands now. Mother and Grace wave. I lean forward in the back seat of the taxi and wave back. 'Thank heaven that's over,' I am saying behind my smile.

The man is unlocking the door. I have had to talk and smile too much in his car, and as I wait I consciously rest my face.

He throws open the door, holds it back with one arm fully extended.

'After you, Mrs Roche.'

'Porteous,' I say. Not that it matters.

'Porteous. Of course. Sorry.'

'Oh,' I say, 'the big black hall-stand is still here.'

'Oh yes,' he says. 'Still here.'

I enter the hall, finding the echoes immediately familiar, and he falls in behind me, coughing rather respectfully. Through the long mirror of the big black hall stand I see a shape pass. It is the shape of an old woman who began to call herself old before she really was, partly to get in first and partly out of a fastidious-ness about the word 'elderly', but who is now really old. She has allowed her shoulders to slump. I press back my shoulders and make first for the living room.

Definitely, I have hopes of the living room.

The man hurries ahead of me and throws open the door. We go in together. We both stop, and look largely around us.

And where now are my hopes?

'Well,' says the man, 'here you are.'

'Yes, here I am.'

By the tone of my voice, its sepulchral parody of doom, I know I have begun again to address my friends at number six. I warn myself to keep this game a private one, because I see that the man, who is looking about him with an almost liquid senti-mentality, has put himself in my place, has taken upon himself the emotions of this 'home-coming', and I do not wish to offend him by my bitter jokes.

'You have a sit-down, eh?' he says. 'While I start getting your ports up.'

I speak before I can stop myself. 'Wait!'

'What,' he says, 'what is it?'

'No. No, it's all right. It's nothing.'

'Right-oh, then.' And off he goes.

Now, suppose I had said, 'Wait, I'm not staying.' What then? The train back to Sydney, and the plane back to London? Impossible. The household at number six is exploded. Exploded. Back only to Sydney then? No. I feel again the utter passivity, the relinquishment of the will to fate, that Hilda and Liza and I all felt on the way back to London from Coventry.

Here I am, and here I will stay. Anything else is too much trouble.

All the same, I admit flatly at last that if I had remembered the house better I would have found some other solution, but the passage of time so blurred and modified it that for these last ten or fifteen years it has been only a sort of squarish blob on my memory. It wasn't until I was on the plane from London that I really saw it again. I had reached that point of sleeplessness, my eyeballs burning behind dry lids, when, without warning, I saw it imprinted on the darkness—no blob now, but *it*, the real house, a heavy wooden box stuck twelve feet in the air on posts. In my confusion and misery I longed painfully for my friends at number six, Hilda and Fred and Liza and poor Belle. I enfolded my right hand about the scratch on my wrist, and as I blinked to lubricate my eyeballs I became incredulously aware of myself sitting in that enormous hollow metal projectile, hemmed in by a host of propped or lolling bodies, listening to those gloomy engines and moving on and on and on through the dark sky.

A suitcase thuds to the floor behind me.

'That's one of them up.'

I turn round. 'Thank you.'

He comes into the room, knocks with a knuckle on the wall. 'Grace,' he says, 'Grace, now, always reckoned this room was practically the same as when you were girls.'

'Yes'.

'Well, this won't get the rest of them up, will it?' And off he goes again.

At my nephew's house in Sydney, they told me that when Grace took over the house from our mother, she had had many renovations done, but had never 'got round' to the living room. 'All the better,' said my nephew's wife. 'You'll be able to do it yourself.' But really, I can't think of a thing that would help this room. It is a room of such a hopeless character that as I look about me I begin to feel a sort of satisfaction. When my worst expectations are met, I frequently find alleviation in detaching myself from the action, as it were, the better to appreciate the addition of one more right, inevitable accent to the pattern of doom, or comedy, or whatever you like to call it. But even as I look about me, and nod, and smile, and say 'Precisely!' I am conscious of a deepening mystification. Because where, in heaven's name, in this room, could have been the source of the exaltation I felt last night on the train?

In Sydney my nephew and his wife often talked of the house, but they talked of so much else, and took me about so much, and I was forced to exclaim and comment so much, that I managed to stave off all concentrated thought of it. I was happy to let it become a blob again. But in the train last night I forced myself to dwell on it, and it was then that my thoughts found a focus in this room, and I was touched by exaltation.

Exaltation? Well, bliss. An obscure sensation, it touched me lightly, the ghost, perhaps, of some former bliss. There is certainly nothing in this room to account for it, so it must have been something outside it, but visible from it.

I hear the thud of another suitcase. He comes in and puts his hands on his hips.

'That's number two.'

'Thank you. So kind.'

'Only a few odds and ends now.'

'That's good. Do you know, I hardly dare to part those curtains.'

'What? Why not?'

He is startled. I have half-shut my eyes and am waggling a finger at eyebrow level. I remind myself again that such little joking habits, fostered in the intimacy of number six, do not travel well. In Sydney my nephew's wife and children, and occasionally even my dear nephew himself, would sometimes give me the same look that this man is giving me now. Smiling, but slightly askance, slightly embarrassed. I am beginning to see our little coterie at number six through other eyes. We would often say to each other, describing incidents that had happened 'outside', 'Oh, he thought me *quite mad*.' It was our happy assumption that everyone in the outside world thought us *quite mad*. But now I am finding that when one is really outside, and alone, it is less of a burden (and much more private) to be thought *quite ordinary*. Besides, I am too tired at present to insist upon my madness. So I lower my hand, and speak in a sensible and reassuring voice.

'Oh, the view, you know. I'm sure it was rather nice from this room. And I'm so afraid it will have changed.'

'The view? Well, there's the cabbage-tree palm . . . the road . . . But you saw all that,' he says, 'as we came in.'

'But not from up here.' I go towards the window. 'I'm sure it was better from up here.'

I am short, he is tall. He comes quickly behind me and pulls the curtains apart. I raise the blind and look through the glass at the leaves of the palm tree. My gaze travels down its trunk, as tall and straight as the electricity poles in the street, and moves over the parched grass. There is drought here—I heard about it in the man's car—and the grass is rather a subtle and gentle colour, a greenish-blond. But that is not what I am looking for.

I look at the dusty shrubs along the fence, I watch two cars pass, then I look up, for a change, at the perfectly plain, sky-blue sky.

'You must be thinking of the flower-beds that used to be there,' I hear him say.

I shake my head.

'Gerberas?' he suggests enticingly. 'Iceland poppies?'

But no, I am not looking for gerberas or Iceland poppies.

'There must have been something else there then,' he says, 'that stuck in your mind. A tree or something.'

'Yes,' I say. There is no need for him to go on. Things are turning out so badly that I am filled again with my perverse contentment.

'Something that died.'

Naturally! If it were a source of delight it *would* have died! Nodding and smiling, I turn back into the room and look about me in the clearer light. On one of the little leggy tables stands a vase of yellow daisies. The vase is too big for them, and they have slipped down to water level with their poor little faces up-raised, like drowning people crying for help. But all the same, someone has taken the trouble to put them there.

I touch the vase. 'What pretty flowers.'

'The wife put them there.'

'How kind. Do thank her.'

'I will, Mrs Roche. Sorry, Porteous. It's that I'm so used to hearing you called Nora Roche. Grace, now, Grace was Grace Chiddy because she went on living here after she was married. But you, round here you still go by your maiden name.'

I have shut my eyes out of sheer weariness, and in one of my sudden severances of attention (accompanied as usual by an expansion in the head) I find myself earnestly pondering the derivation of the term 'maiden name'. 'The name,' I want to say to someone, 'I had when I was a maiden.' I very nearly whisper the words. I open my eyes in fright. Did I in fact whisper them?

No. The man's face is unchanged.

All the same, unless I have a warm bath very soon, and lie down, something regrettable is bound to happen. I take off my hat.

'Well,' I say, 'thank you very much.' And in lieu of his name I add, 'for everything.'

'No trouble. No trouble at all. What kind of a job do you reckon they made of the cleaning?'

'Very good.'

'It was one of those cleaning teams did it.' He bends with his hands on his knees and looks at the legs of a chair. 'Bit of dust there. But generally speaking, they didn't make too bad a fist of it. Not too bad at all. Peter rang, you know. He rang STD and asked me to get one of those professional teams in. So I did.'

Peter is Peter Chiddy, my nephew in Sydney. I wish I could recall the name of this man, but I am too tired, and too ashamed of my discourtesy in having forgotten it, to ask him to repeat it. I don't even know why he met me at the railway station. In the meantime I shall just have to assume that all these services were arranged by my nephew. I can't be bothered reconciling them with his written instructions (lost) to take a taxi to such and such a number in the old street, where I would find this good neighbour (named in the lost instructions) who had the keys, and would let me in.

Now he is saying, 'Oh, and before I forget, the wife thought, the wife said, would you like to come along tonight, and have a bite to eat with us?'

I manage to smile. 'So kind, and do thank her. But I'm much too tired.'

'Fair enough. She thought you might be. So she left a bit of tucker in the kitchen, just in case. And she said she'll be along in the morning to say hello.'

'That will be lovely. And now, what I would like most in the world is a big warm bath.'

'Fair enough. I'll just get that airlines bag, and those books and things, then I'll push off.'

'Thank you, Mr ...' And now I am forced to say, 'I'm so sorry, I've forgotten your name.'

'Cust.'

'Cust. Well, thank you, Mr Cust.'

But now he says, 'You don't remember me, do you, Mrs Porteous?'

I shake my head.

'You don't remember the Custs at all?' he asks incredulously. 'The Custs, in the corner house, the big white one, with the poinciana trees?'

And now, remembering, I look fixedly at the wall beyond his head. 'There were some Custs,' I say with difficulty, like a medium at a séance, 'who had the newsagency.'

'That's me! That's us!' Then he says, 'Or was.'

Still in my trance, I say, 'I worked there for a few months.'

'Right. I was only a little chap then, of course.'

'You used to practise piano scales in the room above the shop.'

He begins to speak, but such trances must not be interrupted. I raise a hand. 'Wait. I have just remembered your maiden name. I mean,' I continue without a blink, 'your Christian name. Jack.'

'Yes, Jack.'

And now he has thrust his head forward and is looking at me closely. I hate being looked at closely. My husband used to do it. Suddenly I am furious with this man Jack Cust, furious with him for his cushiony obtuseness and even for his kindness. I shut my eyes tight. His voice sounds very close.

'Mrs Porteous, you're done in, aren't you?'

I can only nod.

'Look, I'm sorry. I'm really sorry. Standing gasbagging! I'll get those odds and ends up and then I'll really push off.'

As soon as he goes I sit down hard in the straight-backed chair by the window. It goes without saying that never, never in my life, have I chosen the right clothes for a journey. I am hot in all my silly wool. As I take off my jacket Jack Cust comes back, almost running this time, and looking at me anxiously, as if I may be going to beat him.

'Where do you want them, Mrs Porteous?'

'Just there, thank you, Mr Cust.'

His anxiety changes to indignation. 'But the front bedroom's all fixed up for you.'

'Then please, put everything in there.'

He does. He does that. And at last he goes.

It is wonderful to be able to stop smiling. I feel that ever since setting foot in Australia I have been smiling, and saying, 'Thank you' and 'So kind'. I have one rather contemptible characteristic. In fact, I have many. But never mind the others now. The one I am talking about is my tendency to be a bit of a toady. Whenever I am in an insecure position, that is what happens. I massage the smile from my face by pressing the flesh with my fingertips, over and over again, as I used to do when I had that facelift, all those years ago. I long more than ever for that hot bath, but am too tired to move. I am troubled, too, by guilt, because I was irritable with Jack Cust, who was so kind. I shut my eyes, and when, after a few minutes, I open them again, I find myself looking through the glass on to a miniature landscape of mountains and valleys with a tiny castle, weird and ruined, set on one slope.

That is what I was looking for. But it is not richly green, as it used to be in the queer drenched golden light after the January rains, when these distortions in the cheap thick glass gave me my first intimation of a country as beautiful as those in my childhood books. I would kneel on a chair by this window, and after finding the required angle of vision, such as I found just now by accident, I would keep very still, afraid to move lest I lose it. I was deeply engrossed by those miniature landscapes, green, wet, romantic, with silver serpentine rivulets, and flashing lakes, and castles moulded out of any old stick or stone. I believe they enchanted me. Kneeling on that chair, I was scarcely present at all. My other landscape had absorbed me. And later, when I was mad about poetry, and I read *The Idylls of the King* and *The Lady of Shalott*, and so on and so forth, I already had my Camelot. I no longer looked through the glass. I no longer needed to. In fact, to do so would have broken rather than sustained the spell, because that landscape had become a region of my mind, where infinite expansion was possible, and where no obtrusion, such as the discomfort of knees imprinted by the cane of a chair, or a magpie alighting on the grass and shattering the miniature scale, could prevent the emergence of Sir Lancelot.

> From underneath his helmet flowed
> His coal-black curls as on he rode,
>   As he rode down to Camelot.
> From the bank and from the river
> He flashed into the crystal mirror,
> 'Tirra lirra,' by the river
>   Sang Sir Lancelot.

The book was one of my father's. It used to open at the right page because I had marked the place with a twist of silkworm flops, a limp and elongated figure-of-eight. Many readings must have been necessary to drive it into my mind so that I still retain it, because I was—am—a person of undisciplined mind, and in spite of the passion I had for poetry, I could seldom hold more than a few consecutive lines in my head. The poetry in my head was like a jumble of broken jewellery. Couplets, fragments, bits of bright alliteration, and some dark assonance. These, like Sir Lancelot's helmet and his helmet feather, burned like one burning flame together. Often, I used to walk by the river, the real river half a mile from the house. It was broad, brown, and strong, and as I walked beside it I hardly saw it, and never used it as a location for my dreams. Sometimes it overran its banks, and when the flood water receded, mud would be left in all the broad hollows and narrow clefts of the river flats. As soon as this mud became firm, short soft thick tender grass would appear on its surface, making on the green paddocks streaks and ovals of a richer green. One moonlit night, coming home across the paddocks from Olive Partridge's house, I threw down my music case, dropped to the ground, and let myself roll into one of these clefts. I unbuttoned my blouse, unlaced my bodice, and rolled over and over in the sweet grass. I lay on my back and looked first at the moon, then down my cheeks at the peaks of my breasts. My breasts did not have (nor did they ever develop) obtrusive nipples, but the moon was so bright that I could clearly distinguish the two pink discs that surmounted them. I fell into a prolonged trance. I heard the sound of trampling and tearing, but it seemed to come from a long way off. I was astonished when I saw the horse moving along the edge of the cleft. I see him now, a big bay, walking slowly and pulling grass with thievish and desperate-looking jerks of his head. When he had passed I jumped to my feet and quickly laced my bodice. I buttoned my blouse and tucked it into my skirt. My brown hair ribbon lay shining on the grass where my head had been. It was before I put my hair up. I must have been less than sixteen.

I wish I had recalled the incident earlier. I should have liked to have recounted it at number six. It would have had to be told at a time when Fred was not there. Fred had that horror of what he called 'fuggy female talk', and although he made a great comedy of it, we all knew that those exaggerated sour mouths, and all that hissing and head-ducking, covered a real detestation, and so we were careful to spare him. No, I should never have recounted the incident in his presence. It would have been told when he was out, or downstairs, and we three were gossiping in Liza's quarters, perhaps, before her new electric fire. And after I had finished, I know what Hilda and Liza would have said. I can hear Liza's voice, with its touch of dogmatism.

'Of course, Nora, you were looking for a lover.'

And Hilda. 'But of course! As girls did in those days, without even knowing it.'

And I would probably have said, yes, of course, because in these times, when sexuality is so very fashionable, it is easy to believe that it underlies all our actions. But really, though I am quite aware of the sexual nature of the incident, I don't believe I was looking for a lover. Or not only for a lover. I believe I was also trying to match that region of my mind, Camelot.

If that sounds laughable, do consider that this was a long time ago, and that I was a backward and innocent girl, living in a backward and unworldly place. And consider, too, that the very repression of sex, though it produced so much that was warped and ugly and cruel, let loose for some natures, briefly, a luminosity, a glow, that I expect is unimaginable now, and that for those natures, it was possible to love and value that glow far beyond the fire that was its origin.

I am going to put down a strange word. Beauty. I was in love with beauty. I carried my pale face, my dropped flag of ashen hair, my abstracted eyes, my damp concealed body, along the rough roads and streets, and across the paddocks and vacant lots and playing fields, of a raw ugly sprawling suburb on the outskirts of a raw but genteel town. I walked everywhere, oppressed, moody, yet patient too. Our suburb merged with farms, and by day, overtaken by a farmer's cart, I would see the whip flick the horse's rump and the shadow of the cart draw away from a shining pile of excrement. On certain hot nights scents and stench would mingle—frangipani and lantana with the wake of the nightcart. I walked and walked, sometimes with an objective—a friend's house, a shop, the church or school—but mostly at random, to outrun oppression.

I had a pinkish skin that always looked damp and often was. In the swampy summers I sweated dreadfully. I changed my dress-shields three or four times a day and washed them secretly. Most of my friends were dry-skinned girls with suntanned hands and electrical energy. I remember how Olive Partridge would break suddenly into a run, then as suddenly stop and clack her boots together sideways. But though Olive did things like that when she and I were alone, she was dignified in groups and would not play games. She was never present at those tennis afternoons (called 'the tennis'), when the girls staggered from the court and flopped panting on to the grass, and the boys flopped down beside them and splashed their faces with water from the canvas bags. Ashamed of my sweat, I sat alone in the tennis shed. The girls laughed and shrieked, and I could hear the swishing of cloth as they kicked their legs in their skirts and petticoats. My laughter at the antics of the girls was strained, but in a longing for solidarity I eagerly unhooked the water bag and passed it to the boys. My first touch of toadiness?

On Sundays Grace's voice would rout me out of my hiding places.

'Nor-ah! Chur-urch! Church, Nora.'

Our clergyman was a tired man of mechanical piety, and on hot days our little timber church smelled of coconut oil and the petrol used to clean serge suits. Even so, some were devout. Grace was. But not me—I could not worship there. I was no longer a schoolgirl. I walked home from church in a group of girls followed by boys who would lag behind at first, and then, in a sudden burst, run to overtake us. They would jeer and guffaw as they passed, and bump us as if by accident. Some of the girls would send after them shouts of derision mingled with disappointment, and the rest would giggle. Between the guffaw and the giggle there is little to choose, but the guffaw is louder, and to me it carried a threat of cruelty.

Four of these boys formed a regular group. At our houses on singing nights, these four were stiff and proper in their blue serge suits, and polite and shy with our parents, and if we girls encountered one of them alone, he would be much the same, clumsy and shy and anxious to escape. But when these four were together, waiting for us in the dark under the camphor laurels west of the school, though they were awkward at first (apart from the guffaws that broke startlingly out), if they could entice or trick one of us away from the others, they would grab us and throw us to the ground. They would try to pull down our pants one minute and abjectly beg the next. As we made our escape they would villify us horribly.

Nobody was raped. Escape was optional, and for me, in spite of my sexual excitement, imperative. I hated being pulled about and roughly handled. It made me bored and grieved and angry.

'What did you come for then?'

I saw sense in the question, and stopped going. Those girls who continued to go began to treat me with enmity, and for the first time I took note of an ominous growled-out question.

'Who does she think *she* is?'

My retreat took me into another group of boys, friends of my brother Peter, who was older than I but younger than Grace. These were always spoken of as 'thoroughly decent lads', and with them, as I stitched on their cricket pockets or helped to sort their stamp collections, I found boredom of a different sort—plain, you might say, instead of a bit fancy. I withdrew still further. Except for Olive Partridge, who shared my passion for reading, and whose mother looked at me with a kind of quizzical understanding, all my friends became acquaintances. Like almost everybody in those days, I spent a great deal of time in making things with my hands. I made drawings of flowers, and of thin ladies and gentlemen in medieval garments. I did crochet work, embroidery, and made all my own clothes. I read much poetry, and prose of the bejewelled sort. And I walked. I walked. Indeed if all the marks of my walking feet had been left inscribed on the paddocks and roads and playing fields of that suburb, you would have seen lines, arcs, ovals, rectangles, figures-of-eight, and any other shape you might care to name, all imposed and impinging on one another so thickly that it would have been impossible to trace a single journey.

Often, on these walks, I would meet Dorothy Irey. She was a friend of Grace's, six years older than I, and was said to have Polynesian blood. She did not walk fast like I did, but stepped out very absently and gently, her neck stretched high, her head turning this way and that, and her fingertips, meeting at waist level, moving and nibbling together. She was so slender and narrow-hipped, and the rounded mass of her hair, surmounted by a 'mushroom' hat, made her head look so disproportion-ately big, that in the distance she made me think of a poppy, a nodding, advancing poppy. She would smile at me when we were still a long way apart, and as we drew nearer her smile would gradually grow wide and she would call with sing-song condescension, 'Hello, Nora.' And as I replied we would look with appreciation, with secret sharp recognition, at each other's clothes. The effect she gave, of darkness, freshness, and white lace, left me incredulous. She was rare and beautiful, and she was twenty-three. So why did she stay? My own patience was explained by my underlying conviction that *I* was going. I never

for one moment doubted it. 'Why does Dorothy Irey stay here?'
I asked Grace. But Grace turned on me in a fury. 'We don't all
think we're too good for this place, Lady Muck.'

And then we were in one of our quarrels.

'Mother, don't let Grace call me Lady Muck.'

'Now, girls.'

'Then why is Nora always running the place down?'

'Why is Grace always running *me* down?'

'Girls, girls.'

'Mother, tell Nora that one day she will be punished for
her scorn.'

'It is not scorn. It is not scorn at all.'

My mother considered her knitting. Was the wool khaki?
Was it war-time? I think so.

'Well, Nora, scorn is what it sounds like.'

My mother didn't like me much. I first realized it when I was
about six, and had started school, and had seen other children
with their mothers. 'You don't like me much, do you?' I asked
one afternoon.

'Don't be ridiculous, child. The very idea! Never, never let
me hear you say that again.'

It must have been hard on her, having to pretend. I can't remember feeling deprived, as they say today, or holding it against
her. To tell the truth, I didn't like her much either. Our natures
were antipathetic. It happens more often than is admitted.

I continued to wait, but in my obsessive patient walking I
no longer met Dorothy Irey. She was about to become Dorothy
Rainbow, having engaged herself to marry Bruce Rainbow, who
worked in the Rural Bank, but who was now off to the war. I
looked from her to him, and asked myself, 'But why?' I didn't
dare ask Grace, but at the wedding party I whispered to Olive
Partridge, 'But why?'

Olive shrugged. 'He seems quite nice.'

'But to marry? Would you?'

Olive looked round the room. 'I wouldn't marry any of them. I doubt if I'll marry at all.'

Olive was to come into three hundred pounds a year when she was twenty-five. 'And that very minute,' she would say, 'I'm off.'

But I could only wait. I made lampshades, soldier's socks, beaded purses, and embroidered cushion covers. From beneath my eyebrows, I watched myself raise my arms to amass my hair at the back of my head. With sidelong glances, I turned my head this way and that, but there was no one to see. I made ex-travagantly long scarves, and had nowhere to wear them. I still accepted the waiting, hating it, but so sure of escape that I could wait without panic. I read Keats, Shelley, Ella Wheeler Wilcox, and hundreds of novels, fastening on what fed my obsessions and skimming over what didn't. Olive Partridge tried to make me read Shaw and Wells, but I told her (she reminded me of it years later) that they were 'too grey'.

Blue and gold were my favourite colours. Madonna blue. Metallic gold. I wrote many short poems about my own— exquisite, of course—reactions to natural phenomena. Some of these were published in the Women's Page of the *Courier*. When Grace read them aloud at the breakfast table, I listened for sarcasm, but detected none. Engaged to marry an absent soldier and busy with Dorothy Irey's babies, Grace had be-come less severe about my shortcomings. 'Very artistic,' was all she said. 'Refined' and 'artistic' were words often used about me. I frowned when I heard them; I aspired to something of greater intensity.

My brother was killed in the trenches in France. So was Grace's soldier, and all four of the boys under the camphor lau-rel trees. Poor boys. I can say it now. Distance and death have made me generous. Dorothy Rainbow's husband came back.

When the war was over prices rose. My father, a surveyor in the Lands Department, had died when I was six. We needed money. I went to work for Cust the newsagent.

Cust the newsagent, a tall hovering man like his son, told me twice a week that if it weren't for my widowed mother he would not keep me on. I washed my hair twice a week and brushed it every morning and night. I made white voile dresses with lace insertions, and drew designs for my own embroideries. Self-conscious now of my lonely walking, I turned into side streets rather than meet anyone I knew. Dorothy Rainbow, busy with house and babies, I never saw, but Grace answered my enquiries by saying with the old anger that of course she was happy.

'Why shouldn't she be? She has all any reasonable person could want.'

I no longer thought of Sir Lancelot. The war, and the boys under the camphor laurels, had obliterated him. But perhaps not quite. At intervals all through my life, sometimes at very long intervals, there has flashed on my inner vision the step of a horse, the nod of a plume, and at those times I have been filled for a moment with a strange chaotic grief.

At the Custs' shop one day I wept and wept. Why? I can't remember. But I remember how the skin across my cheekbones was stinging and sore from the pressure of my wet forearms, which were spread on the clammy oilcloth of the Custs' kitchen table. When my weeping lost momentum I heard in its pauses the vacuous up-and-down march of piano scales played with boredom, and from nearby the sound of Mrs Cust scrubbing her hands at the kitchen sink. To soothe me, she spoke sooth-ingly to her husband about the garden at the new house, and what it was doing to her hands. It must have been when the Custs were just about to move from the rooms over the shop to the big white house on the corner. The scales stopped. Both the Custs were looking at me. The rays of their glances penetrated my hair and made medallions of discomfort on my scalp. Did I hear the word 'hysteria', or was it unspoken, but in the air? It is certain that Mrs Cust said to her husband that they must get Nora to make cushions for the new house.

'Though it's a shame to sit on them, they're so pretty.'

I must have thought so too. I abandoned cushion covers for wall hangings, again drawing my own designs. Sometimes I sat over these until two in the morning, and the next day dozed in the stock room of the shop. Not the Custs' shop now, but a shop in town, where I stood behind the counter in a grey smock and sold art materials. 'I always knew Nora would end up doing something artistic,' people said to my mother, and at last I began to panic. I no longer bought embroidery silks or the stuff for dresses. I paid my board to Grace and saved the rest. But this way of escape, so slow, did nothing to quell my panic. Panic would rise without warning in my chest, a bird with wings so strong it seemed they must break the bone.

I still suffered greatly from the heat, and on hot bright nights I would smear my skin with citronella, take a rug, and go and lie on my back on the lawn. All ugliness and panic were then obliterated. I was amazed and enthralled by the thickness and brilliance of the stars, by the rich darkness of the sky, and the ambiguous peacefulness of the blazing moon. In an aureole of turquoise the moon sailed across the sky, and as I watched, our block of land became a raft and began to move, sailing swiftly and smoothly in one direction while the moon and clouds went off in the other. But by this time my illusions were apt to be broken by impatience or self-consciousness, and soon the magic would pall, or I would hear Grace come down from the house, stamping towards me in indignation and crying that I was to come upstairs this very minute.

It is true that this block of land is as flat as a raft. Now that I have moved my head I can no longer see mountains, valleys, and a castle. What I see now is a stone lying on grass that is rather a subtle and gentle colour, a greenish-blond. Many cars are passing in the road. People are coming home from work.

I have sat too long in this hard-backed chair, and as I rise I make the theatrical grimaces of pain with which I used to amuse my friends at number six. On this mantelshelf there was once a photograph of my brother, a boy wearing a thick hairy uniform, thick puttees, thick boots, and an Anzac hat. And another of my father, the fair young photographed face that is my sole recollection of him. But both are gone; the only photograph here now is of mild Tom Chiddy, the widower Grace married when he was fifty-five and she thirty-two. They moved into this house so that Grace could look after my mother, who had broken her hip. But by that time I was married myself, and living in Sydney.

Long before I left, Sydney had stood proxy for Camelot, a substitution forced upon me by what little common sense I had. In fact, all my early fevers seemed to have passed, and in those days I did not know that such infections can enter the blood, or that a tertiary stage is possible.

As I pull down the blinds, and draw the curtains together, I address my friends at number six.

'This is one room I shall never use.'

I hear their replies. 'What of it?' says Liza. 'There are other rooms.'

And Hilda agrees. 'Of course! What luck that the place is so *big*.'

I pick up my jacket and hat. 'What is mere space?' I say as I walk to the door.

'Space?' This time it is Fred. He is excited. He turns on a heel, waves an arm. 'I will tell you. Space is a boon, a property, a positive benefit.'

'You see?' say Hilda and Liza.

'Maybe.' I am in the hall; I shut the door. 'But,' I say as I walk down the hall, 'I am no longer used to space.'

The front bedroom, where Jack Cust has put my things, used to be my mother's room, but it is a spare room now, and to my relief is as neat and negative as a hotel bedroom. I take the flask of brandy from my bag and drink a nip from the screw cap.

In the bathroom I find hot water and sewerage. Sewerage! Never again shall I hide behind a tree or turn in my tracks as the nightcart approaches. Lying in a hot bath, I remember how all the girls went on about the nightman. 'Never let the nightman see your face.' Did we perhaps believe he had the evil eye? One night I hid behind a tree and watched him pass, a thin man, with bowyangs round his trouser legs, who jogged along with the can on one shoulder and the opposite arm held out from his side.

I doze in the bath, but not for long, because the water is still warm when I get out. Yet suddenly I am cold, trembling, and afraid. Is it because I have eaten nothing all day except a little of that peculiar food on the train? I put on a warm gown and go to the kitchen.

I am repelled by the red linoleum, its mottled areas and visceral shine. But on the table, under a plastic dome, I find a plate of sandwiches.

'And look—parsley.'

I am speaking to Liza, who always ate the parsley. Beside the plate is a note.

Have made up bed in spare bedroom. Strawberries and icecream in fridge. Milk ditto. B. Cust.

The kettle is full, the tea things set out beside the stove, and I find a loaf of bread in the crock. And when I open the re-frigerator, and bend to look in, I see a blue-walled interior as comforting as a little lighted house. Strawberries, honey, butter, six eggs, a plate of bacon. How very nice of B. Cust.

Food and hot tea lift my spirits. Somewhere in this house, I say to myself, I shall make my domain. In whatever circumstances I have found myself, I have always managed to devise a little area, camp or covert, that was not too ugly. At times it was a whole room, but at others it may have been only a corner with a handsome chair, or a table and a vase of flowers. Once, it was a bed, a window, and a lemon tree. But always, I have managed to devise it somehow, and no doubt I shall do it again.

I am awakened the next morning by the sound of someone unlocking the front door. Then I hear a voice raised in that female signal of search or warning. 'Oooh-oooh.' On a descending note.

Before I can gather my wits to reply, I hear her footsteps in the hall. And her voice.

'It's all right, Mrs Porteous. It's only me. Mrs Cust.'

My spectacles are not on my bedside table. As I start patting the blankets to find them, she arrives at my open door.

'I did knock,' she says.

'I can't find my spectacles,' I say stupidly.

She approaches the bed. 'Were you using them last night?'

'I think so. Yes, I was. I was reading.'

'They aren't on your bedside table.'

'I know they're not. Whatever is the time?'

'Look, here they are on the floor. And your book too. Good thing they didn't break.'

I put them on and look at my watch. 'Goodness. Eleven o'clock.'

'I know. That's why I thought I had better come in. I came up a while ago, but you didn't answer my knock, so I ran home and got the spare key. I'll leave it with you. You'd better keep it now. And I brought your gloves. You left them in Jack's car.'

She is a tallish brown-skinned woman with thin active-looking legs and grey bouncy hair cut short. She wears a printed cotton dress and an orlon cardigan with knife-edged creases down the sleeves. 'The Brisbane climate is a cardigan climate,' I used to tell them at number six. With an anxious but timid tilt of her head, she asks how I am this morning. I refuse to indulge my exhaustion and reply in a lively manner that I am very well indeed.

'Are you?' she says.

'You sound as if you don't believe me, Mrs Cust.'

'Of course I do.' But she still sounds doubtful. 'Please call me Betty,' she says then.

'So that's what the B stands for? I will call you Betty if you call me Nora.'

'All right—Nora.' She presses on against the tide of her own timidity. 'I was a good friend of Grace's, so I'm used to coming in and out of this house. I hope you didn't mind me just barging in.'

'Not at all. I'm very glad you woke me. Imagine sleeping like that! I wonder if I took two pills instead of one. I think I have a lot to thank you for. This bed, the flowers, the sandwiches.'

My vivacity is irritating even to myself, but I don't seem to be able to stop it. 'Lovely sandwiches. I didn't leave a crumb. I even ate the parsley. And what wonderful strawberries.'

'Local strawberries.' By her abruptness she tries to avert my gratitude. She puts my gloves on the dressing table. 'Aren't these gloves soft?'

'A very good friend gave them to me last Christmas.' I am speaking of Fred, who gave us all a pair—Hilda, Liza and me. For Belle he bought a chain collar with a name tag. I see Belle in the cage, immobile now, her paws drawn neatly beneath her, no longer quivering, but expressionless, withdrawn, refusing to look at me. She is still wearing the chain collar, which disrupts her grey ruff. Flooded by useless grief, I hold my left wrist in my right hand. 'Whose idea was it to meet the train?' I ask.

'Ours.'

'I thought so. Peter told me to get a taxi.'

'That's what he told us, that you'd get a taxi. But I bet he knew perfectly well,' she says in amiable disparagement, 'that we wouldn't let you. Good heavens, Jack's glad to have something to do, now he's retired.'

'Well,' I say, 'it was very good of you both.'

'That's all right. I don't suppose you remember me, do you, Nora?'

'I don't *think* . . .'

'No, well, I was little when you were big. I was Betty Flitcroft.'

'Flitcroft.' I look at the ceiling and fall again into my geneological trance. 'There were some Flitcrofts in Ivanhoe Road.'

'That was us.'

'I went to school with Else Flitcroft. You must be Else's younger sister.'

'Fourteen years younger. Else died last year in Perth. Nora, do you remember the wall hanging you made for mother?'

I move one shoulder in apology. 'I made so many.'

'I know. "One of Nora Roche's embroideries", we say round here. Else used to have ours, but it's mine now. One of these days I'll bring it over to show you.'

I feel an interior cringing from this threatened confrontation. When I made those wall hangings I thought they were marvellous, so it follows that they will be sad bungles. 'That will be lovely,' I say.

'You must have been terribly artistic,' she says. 'So was Grace of course, in another way. She had to let the front garden go, it got too much for her, but she had the back just lovely. It's not much now, of course.'

'I haven't seen it. I haven't even looked at the back rooms yet.'

'Jack said how tired you were. I'll tell you what, you stay there, and let me bring you breakfast on a tray.'

But against my own weariness I pit my need for independence, on which I made such a declaration to my nephew. I make myself look shocked.

'Certainly not! You must think me a wretched, slothful old woman. I'll be up and about in less than ten minutes.'

'Oh, all right,' she says, 'if you prefer. But look, Jack and I are going shopping this morning, so say you make out a list and we'll get you anything you need. Unless you feel like coming with us? We could drive you around and show you how the old place has changed. Not too many of the old families here now, Nora. And the price of a building block! Honestly! And down by the river, all those modern houses. And to think that once upon a time nobody would build there because in eighteen-ninety-something it flooded.'

'Only the Partridges,' I say.

'Oh, old Mrs Partridge is still there. Ninety-five. Think of it! Olive flew back to see her last year, but she only stayed a week, and none of us saw her. Not to talk to, that is. You used to see her in London, Grace said.'

'I did when I first went over.' I am thinking of Olive in the abortionist's waiting room, saying through her teeth that she would rather be anywhere than there. I remember my own curt answer, and I sigh, and say to Betty Cust, 'But later on we lost touch. I don't think I will come with you to the shops, thank you, Betty. But I should certainly be glad of some provisions.'

'Good. Then say I come back for your list in twenty minutes.' She picks up my book, turns a few pages, puts it down. 'Do you like Olive Partridge's books?'

'Very much. Especially the later ones.'

'Those are the ones I can't read. They make me depressed.'

'They make me jealous.'

She gives me that askance look, followed by an uncertain laugh.

'I don't believe it!' she says as she goes.

And indeed, why should she believe it, I crossly ask myself, when it isn't true? The possibility that I have re-entered a milieu in which I shall be compelled to explain my every facetious remark, in which I shall not find even *one person* to whom I can say anything I please, fills me with boredom.

" 'I was only joking", ' Fred once said, 'are the four saddest words in the world.'

So I am irritated with Betty Cust for her lack of perspicacity, and angry with myself for my irritation, because she is so kind. To escape the bonds such kindness imposes, physical independence seems more necessary than ever. But it is amazingly hard to get up. Did I in fact take two pills instead of one? Almost asleep again, I hear, or imagine I hear, a noise like a tennis ball striking a racquet, and suddenly I see myself at the window of Olive's flat in Cadogan Square. They are playing tennis in the square. The trees are in full leaf, and of the players I see only moving patches of lacy white through the green. But how distinctly I hear the percussion of balls against catgut. Even as I force myself awake I fancy I can hear it still, fading away into the vast blue Queensland sky outside.

I force myself out of bed, but find that even to walk to the bathroom I must support myself with a hand against the wall. Behind my ribs there is a strange coldness, heavy, like earth or clay. I no longer want tea. From the bathroom I go straight back to bed. I turn the blanket up high, take a pen and paper from my handbag, and begin my shopping list. But I have not got very far before Betty Cust comes back.

'Oh,' she says at once, 'you do look sick. I knew you were sick.'

'Reaction to the journey.' But suddenly, I have a pain across my chest. 'Unless it's a heart attack,' I say unwillingly.

'I'll get a doctor.'

'I don't really think it's a heart attack.'

'Neither do I. But there's a funny sort of flu going around this year. It might be that. So I'll get a doctor.'

'Are you retired too?'

'Retired?'

'You said Jack is glad to have something to do because he's retired.'

'Nora, don't you want me to get a doctor?'

The fact is, I want her to get one without admitting I need one. 'I feel such a nuisance,' I say feebly.

'Don't say that, Nora. Your phone's not connected yet. I'll run down home and ring him from there.'

She probably can run, too, on those long thin legs. I see her in caricature, bounding so high along the street that her thick grey hair is lifting and falling. It is impossible not to like her. In only a few minutes she is back.

'I got Doctor Smith. He'll come as soon as he can.'

My helplessness has quite cured her shyness. She is brisk and competent. 'Don't bother with that list. We'll get you the basic things.' She puts the back of her hand on my forehead, and we both keep dead quiet for a while, as if expecting some audible result. Then she says, 'H'mmm,' and tucks the bedclothes firmly round me. 'He says that in the meantime you're to stay in bed and keep warm. Are you warm enough? Are you sure? I'll stay here till he comes.'

'No,' I say. And then, to qualify my curtness: 'My dear, what harm can come to me alone? I'll just go to sleep.'

She looks worried, but says, 'All right, if you prefer. I'll leave the front door open for him. He's used to that. And we won't be long anyway.'

As soon as she goes I fall into a fluttering shallow sleep, and when I wake, still alone, I feel again that heavy insistent cold behind my ribs, and wonder if I am about to die. I hold my left wrist in my right hand and reflect that I could hardly have chosen a more appropriate time to die. But this indifference is immediately demolished by a sharp anger. I know this anger well. It concerns Colin Porteous, but is directed less against him than against vile wastage, vile wastage. Feeling very gloomy indeed, I turn my head and see in the sky a white half-moon. It is made of exquisitely thin porcelain but is discoloured where age and use have worn off some of the glaze. Liza used to say that she saw her past life as a string of roughly-graded beads, and so did Hilda have a linear conception of hers, thinking of it as a track with detours. But for some years now I have likened mine to a globe suspended in my head, and ever since the shocking realization that waste is irretrievable, I have been careful not to let this globe spin to expose the nether side on which my marriage has left its multitude of images. This globe is as small as my forehead, yet so huge that its surface is inscribed with thousands, no, millions of images. It is miraculously suspended and will spin in response either to a deliberate turn or an accidental flick. The deliberate turns are meant to keep it in a soothing half-spin with certain chosen parts to the light, but I am not an utter coward, and I don't mind inspecting some of the dark patches now and again. Only I like to manipulate the globe myself. I don't like those accidental flicks. In fact, there are some that I positively dread, and if I see one of these coming, I rush to forestall it, forcing the globe to steadiness so that once more it faces the right way. I have become so expert at this, so watchful and quick, that there is always a nether side to my globe, and on that side flickers and drifts my one-time husband—and, I have often thought, a very good place for him too. But when I say that Colin Porteous is on that side, I mean, of course, the real Colin Porteous, because he has—or do I mean, had—an edited version that I kept on the light side to present to chosen audiences. In fact, at number six he was one of our favourite characters, him and his girl Pearl.

And as well, I have always had an understanding with my-self that my evasion about the real Colin Porteous was to be only temporary, and that one day I would turn the globe round and have a good look at him. It occurs to me now that if I am about to die I have no time to lose. It has sometimes happened that I have kept certain events and persons on the nether side and later have found there to have been no need, no need at all. This house, for example, and those early years of waiting and walking. They have been turned to the light now, and what harm have they done me? It is surely bizarre to suppose that they have made me ill.

Before I can decide the matter I fall into another half-transparent sleep, and this time I am awakened by a man who introduces himself as Doctor Rainbow, and says he has come instead of Doctor Smith, who has been called to a confinement. He is a tall man with a heavy inflexible-looking body, a slow walk, and black, low-growing hair. I want to ask him if he is Dorothy Rainbow's son, but he begins immediately to exam-ine me.

'Breathe. Go-od. Again. Go-od. Now, this side, please. That's right. Breathe . . .'

He takes my temperature, counts my pulse, then pulls down the bedclothes and looks at my legs.

'Feet ever swell?'

'Sometimes.'

'One or both?'

'I've never noticed.'

'Can't be bad then.' He prods the calf of my leg. 'That hurt?'

'I don't think so.'

'If you don't know, it doesn't.' He prods the other calf. 'How about that?'

'No.'

'Ah.'

He sits down and takes his prescription pad from his bag. 'You have pneumonia. Mrs Cust said she will get you anything you need. I'll leave you two prescriptions. Give them to her, please. She'll get them made up. Keep warm, and stay in bed all the time.'

'Why should I get pneumonia? I haven't had a cold.'

He has begun to write and does not reply until he has finished.

'You can get it without that.'

'Why did you look at my legs?'

'Checking for signs of thrombosis. Found none. How did you get that scratch?'

He must have seen it while he was counting my pulse. I pull the cuff of my nightgown over it. 'From a cat.'

'How long ago?'

'Three weeks.'

'It ought to be healed by now. I'll give you something for that as well.'

He sits down and writes again, and as soon as he stops I ask him if he is Dorothy Rainbow's son. He nods and gives me the third prescription.

'I knew her when she was Dorothy Irey.'

He is putting things back in his bag. 'Did you?'

'She was so beautiful,' I say.

He nods again. 'Have you had any operations?'

'A curette.' I always call it a curette. 'But good heavens, so long ago.'

'Any others?'

The facelift is irrelevant; I shan't mention the facelift.

'No.'

'What illnesses?'

'I used to get severe bronchitis. But I haven't had a really bad attack for a long time now. Arthritis is my present worry. Hands.' I display them. 'Elbows. Knees. You must be Dorothy's youngest.'

His failure to reply disconcerts me. He must have heard. Almost timidly I say, 'Aren't you?'

'Yes.'

The word is so reluctant, so guarded and nearly hostile, that it chills me. I stare into his eyes and ask no more questions. But I wonder. When he goes, I begin to wonder. Dorothy died just after the war, so it can't be that I have blundered on the tender spot of a recent bereavement. I try to recall what my mother's letters, and Grace's, told me about Dorothy over the years. It adds up to very little. Bruce Rainbow 'doing so well in the bank', Dorothy's children 'all such nice youngsters', additions to their house making it 'the best home in the street', Dorothy's eldest boy passing an examination 'with flying colours', Dorothy being 'a bit down in the mouth', and Grace taking her to work at the Red Cross, which 'quite took her out of herself'.

These and other phrases were all typical of the letters Grace and my mother wrote to me, and of those I wrote in return, for it seemed that whenever one member of our family sat down to write to another, the very act invoked a spell compelling us to present our lives and our surroundings as utterly, impossibly, banal. There were occasional exceptions, however, when under the attack of some emotion unexpectedly felt while writing, this strange rigidity would relax for a moment, and life would leap in. I recall one such instance now, in a letter of Grace's.

'The Rainbow house is up for sale. It makes me weep to pass it.'

Did I ask for an explanation? I am sure I got none. But then, our later correspondence was so irregular that it was possible for questions to be asked, and then for the questioner to forget even what she had asked.

I go to sleep again, and wake to see Betty and Jack Cust standing in the doorway. He is carrying a carton of groceries, and both are looking at me with serious eyes.

'Has he been?' asks Betty.

'Yes. He says I have pneumonia.'

'That's no good!' says Jack with great heartiness.

'But not too bad either,' says Betty, coming in. 'Not these days.'

Jack goes to the kitchen with the goods. 'Betty,' I say, 'what happened to Dorothy Rainbow?'

'What?' She picks up the prescriptions. 'Oh, I see! It was Gordon Rainbow.'

'He was rather strange.'

She nods. 'Very reserved.'

'No. Strange when I mentioned her.'

'Well, he doesn't.'

'Doesn't mention her?'

'No. Never. It was the shock.'

'Was she killed in an accident?'

The hand holding the prescriptions falls to her side. 'Nora, I don't understand this. You must know about it.'

She gives me no time to say that I don't. 'Grace told you about it, I know that. I remember it distinctly. I came up here one day, and she was writing a letter, and she told me she was writing to you about Dorothy.'

I see myself, not long after the war, picking up a small pile of letters from the mat inside my door, impassively tearing each of them open, crumpling the paper unread, throwing them in the grate. Opening and crumpling them only so that they would burn the better. There had seemed no point in reading them.

'Some mail did go astray about that time,' I tell Betty.

'That must be it then. Never mind about it now. I'll go straight up to the chemist and get these made up. We can talk another time. You're sick.'

'I am sick. Isn't it strange what one forgets to ask doctors. Always something. I forgot to ask if I am dying.'

Does she laugh because she thinks I am joking, or because she thinks I am not? I am really very sick. In the next few days she and Jack come in and out bearing all kinds of offerings— food I can't eat, tea, fruit juices, glucose drinks. Doctor Rainbow looks worried and speaks of sending me to a hospital, but after a consultation in the hall with Betty Cust, he decides to leave me where I am. Two girls in uniforms and panama hats appear beside my bed. I ask them what school they go to, and they laugh and say they aren't schoolgirls, they're district nurses. When I ask them why in that case they wear school hats, they laugh again, and when I tell them that our school hats weren't quite like theirs, but were lined with brown crinoline, they can hardly stop laughing. Next time I see them I recognize them as nurses, and tell them that I don't need to be washed every few hours. But they laugh again, and say that they come only once a day.

Doctor Rainbow is often by my bed.

'Now, breathe . . .'

I tell him I want to ask him something, but have forgotten what it is. 'Then keep on forgetting it,' he says. 'Come along now. Breathe . . .'

Apart from the laughing nurses, I see another young woman. She has inquisitive eyes and a big mouth with a simian bulge. I watch her as she stands with her back to me, examining my hair brushes and toilet articles. As if feeling my eyes on her, she turns suddenly. I shut my eyes and pretend to sleep.

At times I am detached from the scene about me, and yet perceive it with a greatly heightened lucidity. Betty Cust sits in a cane chair. She knits, she darns socks. Jack Cust passes the door, or frowns as he unwraps a parcel of medicine. They seem close and brightly lit, yet too distant to address. It is like being in a stationary train at night, making a chink in the blind of one's sleeper and seeing people standing in a waiting room as bright as day. Only a few yards away, but unreachable. It is like that. The white porcelain moon is growing, but I never see the yellow moon at night. I watch the white daytime moon, and in the very next second, it seems, I open my eyes and see a dark sky and a few weak stars.

It becomes possible to reach and speak to the people about me, but I hear myself saying irrational things.

'What has happened to all the stars, Mr Cust?'

'It's the electricity, Mrs Porteous.'

'But stars aren't worked by electricity, Mr Cust.'

'I mean the electricity down here, Mrs Porteous.'

One night I put on my spectacles and the stars become thicker and brighter, but still, not nearly as thick and bright as they used to be.

'It used to be a great blaze,' I tell Betty Cust. 'I found it hypnotic when I was a girl. I used to lie on my back on the grass and stare and stare. You've no idea how cross it made Grace.'

Betty holds her knitting up and regards it seriously. Fred used to say he couldn't bear people who never say anything nasty about anyone else. 'That mixture is too bland,' he would say in his explosive way. Betty continues with her knitting. 'Grace altered such a lot towards the end of her life, Nora.'

There is a reflective grief in her voice. The mixture is not too bland. And nor is there evidence of another of Fred's bugbears—the sugar that hides the evil taste.

The white moon becomes a full disc. 'If you don't respond better than this,' says Doctor Rainbow, 'it will be hospital after all.' To avoid hospital, I compel myself to vivacity, and almost immediately begin to feel better. The wound on my wrist no longer displays its thread of blood, and I begin to write to Hilda and Liza in my head.

My dears, I am sick, and have an enormous glum doctor on the model of Frankenstein's monster . . .

I have had no letters from Hilda and Liza. There is a mail strike. I read about it in the newspaper each morning. I hold this paper in a gingerly manner because much ink comes off on my fingers.

'I'm sure it is a splendid newspaper,' I say to Lyn Wilmot. 'So nice and black.'

Lyn Wilmot is the young woman I saw examining my hair brushes. She reminds me—I realize it suddenly—of Una Porteous. She has an unfortunate effect on me. I am a toady in her presence, thanking her too much and suavely admiring her hair and her dresses. She is my next door neighbour, and Betty has engaged her to come in twice a day.

'She needs the money, Nora. Her husband's on strike, and with two children they're going through a hard patch.'

So what could I say?

Young, strong, and fat behind the knees, Lyn Wilmot takes off her cardigan and in a short dress of orange and cyclamen cotton very slowly dusts my room.

'I don't suppose I should say this, but I don't like Doctor Rainbow. Doctor Smith's the one I like.'

She lingers over each object she touches, sometimes forgetting me in her engrossment. But at other times she remembers me, and looks at me two or three times, rapid reflective glances, before speaking.

'I wonder if you'll find money goes further here than in London.'

'I'm sure I hope so.'

'Things are dear here.'

'And there.'

'They say it's hard on pensioners here.'

'I suppose it is.'

'But of course, if your husband left you comfortably off ...'

I say nothing. If she wants to know, she will have to ask.

She shifts my handbag. 'You have nice things.' She hums a scrap of a tune. *Dee-di-dee.* 'And actually how long have you *been* a widow, Mrs Porteous?'

'I am not a widow, Mrs Wilmot.'

'Oh?' she says. She gives me plenty of time, but I say nothing. 'What are you then?' she blurts out.

'I am a divorcée.'

She makes a long-drawn guttural noise, inquisitive yet knowing—such a familiar noise that I can't resist telling her at last how much she reminds me of my former mother-in-law.

'Una Porteous was a very fine woman,' I say piously.

The sugar that hides the evil taste. 'But that's different,' Fred would have said. 'You know you're doing it.' It would be possible to maintain that I am all the worse for that, but Fred always made infinite allowances for his friends. For them he would topple all his preferences, and turn his opinions inside-out. Which is why the débâcle in April was such a shock to us all.

Lyn Wilmot's duster, which looks to me like an old singlet of her husband's, lags meditatively on my dressing table. 'Actually how long were you married for then?'

'My dear girl, I would have to work it out, and I am much too sick. What pretty colours in your frock.'

That night, feeling safe and detached, and relishing my weakness in the warm bed, I remind myself of my mortality and determine on an inspection of Colin Porteous. Having always assumed that I would only have to take this decision to

make the globe whizz round, I am disconcerted when all I see
is the usual figure, the version I edited for the entertainment of
my friends.

'The substitute,' I say aloud. And immediately, the globe
turns. I see Colin Porteous, with camels and pyramids behind
his fair head, smiling and checking by touch the corner of a
handkerchief protruding from his breast pocket. I know I must
be there too, facing him for the first time, but instead I materi-
alize in the garden of the house he stands in, so that he, like an
actor improvising to cover the late entrance of another, must
continue to smile, and touch his white handkerchief, while I approach through the garden. The house, at Southport, belongs to
Olive Partridge's aunt, and the occasion is Olive's farewell party.
Next week she sails for Europe. I am wearing a sleeveless dress
of apricot georgette and I am hurrying back from the lavatory
to the dancing. The house is a flimsy box shaking with music
and set with yellow squares which are crossed and re-crossed
by rapidly jogging heads and torsos. The jacaranda boughs are
swinging and the paper festoons and streamers on the verandah
are trilling and fluttering in the ocean wind. Suddenly infected,
too exalted to blink, I leap on to the low verandah and rush
into the hall. But here are people, perhaps twenty, grouped in
twos and threes, talking. I am slowed down at once by their im-
mobility, and become stupid and blundering. Still, I will dance.
I am making my way through them towards the dancing when
I come face to face with a dark man, thin and not young. I see
him standing with one foot extended, reaching with a thumb
and forefinger into the pocket of his waistcoat. He draws something out, perhaps a watch. 'Why are you looking at me with
such horror?' he asks.

He knew it was not horror. His voice was low, the look in
his eyes like a caught breath. I turned and ran, flaming with fear
and excitement, into the big bedroom set apart for the girls. I

stood in the centre of the floor, beating a fist against my mouth and saying softly, 'Oh, oh, oh, oh, oh.' Then I made up my mind, bent swiftly to the mirror to look once into my own eyes, and ran back to find him again.

But where he had been standing, I found another man, similar but younger, and fair instead of dark. He was smiling, and touching with two fingers the handkerchief in his breast pocket. Behind his head was a picture of camels and pyramids. 'Are you looking for someone?' he asked.

'That man ...' I could not go on. I was confused because it seemed like a deliberate trick of substitution.

'What man?'

'The man who was here.'

'You must mean John Porteous,' said the fair man. 'He's my uncle. I'm Colin Porteous. We've both been putting up next door with my other uncle. And I still am, if that interests you.'

I said nothing. I wanted to ask where John Porteous had gone, but I was afraid of the fair man's mockery, and did not dare.

'I knew it was him you came back to find,' said Colin Porteous. 'I could tell by the way you looked at him.'

'How do you know how I looked at him?' I asked furiously.

'Because I was standing here beside him.'

I started. 'I didn't see you.'

'I know you didn't. Eyes,' he said, 'only for him.'

'I wanted to ask him something,' I said. 'That's why I came back.'

'Ask me instead.'

'I want to ask him.'

'I'm sorry. He's gone.'

'But it's early. Won't he be back?'

'Back from India? I don't think so.'

'You're joking about India.'

'No. He sails at eleven forty-five. If you run out to the gate you might just see the tail lights of my other uncle's car.'

I couldn't speak. He came a step nearer and looked closely into my face. 'Well, well, well. My, oh, my.'

The sky was red behind the two camels, the pyramids, and the third camel now revealed to me by the forward thrust of Colin Porteous's head. I studied them earnestly while he softly stroked my arm.

'Do you know who you're like?'

If I did, I would not say.

'Lillian Gish. With your hair down, I bet you look just like Lillian Gish. Dance? I'm not my uncle, of course, but at least I'm not married. And I'm a darn sight younger, too. He's forty-five.'

I was twenty-five. You wouldn't think a woman of twenty-five would go on like that, would you? But that is what happened. Colin Porteous was a lawyer who worked for the New South Wales government. After his first call on me, my mother looked at me with respect, and Grace, her brows raised and her mouth awry, called him 'Prince Charming himself'.

'At last,' she said, 'you will have a chance to leave this hateful place.'

'I have never called it hateful. Never.'

'Never out loud.'

'Girls, girls.'

'You may not have noticed, mother,' said Grace, 'but I am no longer a girl. I am thirty-one.'

As a signal of approval he was asked to dinner. With the port wine (for him alone), my father's photograph was brought out.

But it was I who looked at it with curiosity, who took it from his hands and carried it to the light. 'I can't remember one single thing about him,' I said in wonder.

'How old were you when he . . .' asked Colin.

'Six,' replied my mother, taking the photograph from me.

'Old enough to remember,' said Colin, and added in his 'teasing' voice, 'I hope you are not heartless.'

Although the silence of my mother and Grace may have implied that I was, nothing could deflect him from his covetousness of me. Having lost confidence in my own attraction, I could not imagine what I had done to deserve it. We were married before he returned to Sydney.

'A whirlwind *ro*-mance,' said Una Porteous in her slow grating voice. Colin was annoyed because his brother, with his wife and three children, had moved into Una's house in his absence, and had left no room for us.

'A man goes away for a break,' he said, 'and comes back to find himself ousted.'

'Well, Col, if you had of come back alone, naturally you would of had your old room back and no argument. We could squeeze one in even now, but to squeeze two in wouldn't be fair to anyone, least of all to Nora, who will be wanting her own little place. Of course if I had of known you was getting married, Col. But I was not informed. I don't know how I was expected to know, when I was not informed.'

It was a red-brick house in a big flat chequerboard suburb, predominately iron-grey and terracotta in colour, and treeless except for an occasional row of tristanias, clipped to roundness and stuck like toffee apples into the pavement. 'If I had to live here I would die,' I told Colin.

'Die?'

He had just come home from work and we were getting ready to go to Una Porteous's house for dinner. While we looked for a small flat he had found board for us both in the same street. 'Die?' he said, combing his hair in the mirror.

'Oh, of course I don't mean *die*. What I mean is, it's not like Sydney.'

'What *is* like Sydney?'

'The harbour.'

'You won't find a flat near the harbour, not one I can afford.'

But he was wrong. He had never looked. I found one in an old house with a waterfront garden, and begged Colin to take it. He was in love with me then, and besides, he could save on fares by walking over Wolloomooloo and the Domain to his department in the city.

The old house was one of four on Potts Point. I remember their names. Bomera. Tarana. Crecy. Agincourt. In Sydney recently my nephew offered to take me there, but I had already looked across at Potts Point through his binoculars, and had seen Bomera and Tarana joined to Garden Island by an ugly, car-infested concrete isthmus. Garden Island was a real island then, with a few little battleships mooning about like the navy of Ruritania. The four houses stood opposite. One, Bomera, was of stone, built by convicts, and the other three were early Victorian. Ours was Crecy. I could not find it through my nephew's binoculars. Our flat was only one big room with a kitchen and bath, but the big room was very big indeed, with a high ceiling, a north aspect, and three pairs of long double windows through which one saw people, flowers, cats, water, sky, seagulls, ships. It was furnished with some old unimportant pleasant things, and it has remained for me a pattern of what a room should be.

When one falls in love with a city, it is always with only a part of it. 'My' Sydney, of which the houses on the point were the heart, was bound on the north by the harbour, on the south by Bayswater Road, on the west by the city (some of which it included), and on the east by Beach Road at Rushcutters Bay. In this Sydney I became conscious for the first time of the points of the compass, and felt for the first time the airs of three other climates, borne on to my skin by the three prevailing winds. In this limited territory I was very happy in spite of my sexual difficulties.

I do not propose to add to the documents on coition, but it does seem necessary to say that for a long time I got no more enjoyment from it than I had from the mangling and pulling about by the boys under the camphor laurels, of whose activities it seemed a simple but distressing extension. Perhaps I had waited too long. 'Do this,' Colin Porteous would say. 'Do that.' And I would do this and that, and not know whether to laugh or cry in my misery.

He was always very amiable about it. 'Well, you're frigid, and that's that. Women with your colouring are often frigid.' And he would go on to tell me about 'passionate Spanish women' and 'experienced French women' in a way that I knew perfectly was puerile, though I would not let myself admit it lest it undermine my determination to be in love with him. The first substitute I made for him was a man I could love, and in this I was greatly supported by the happiness of my life while he was at work.

I suppose many women of my generation can recall a similar delicious period, when one's idleness and play are without guilt because 'it is only until the children come'. Bomera had a shifting population of which the two stable elements were a dressmaker, Ida Mayo, and a gentle bearded watercolourist in a grey dustcoat, whose name I have forgotten. At any given time, the rest would be mostly artists and actors, but one might also find a restaurant cook, a remittance man, a clerk or an engineer. The old carriage drive led from the gatehouse to a portico under a magnolia tree. This portico was square, with a broad balustrade suitable for sitting on, and opened on to a wide hall with a floor of white marble. Across the hall two statues faced each other. One, Wisdom, held a book in her hand, and the other, Folly, held, I think, a bunch of grapes. The double front doors stood open day and night, and at whatever time I went there, I always found someone about and was sure of a welcome. I would talk to them, pose for them, drink their coffee, listen to their music, and borrow their books. I began by trying to match their sophistication (as it seemed to me then), but they soon detected my ignorance, and took pleasure in startling and shocking me. I took the cue, and to please them, pretended to be even more ignorant than I was, covering my face and giving a dramatic cry, or putting my hands over my ears and begging them to stop. Amused by this game, they began to treat me with a sort of teasing condescension, as if I were a toy, almost a mascot. Only Ida Mayo the dressmaker refused to be amused.

'The fact is, Nora knows more about colour than any of you lot, with your daubs.'

Ida was a specialist, her card said, in evening wear. I was impressed by her skill, and enjoyed helping her. Colin held the opinion, common in those days, that a man was disgraced if his wife worked for money, and with Ida I had occupation without disgrace. Her two rooms were dimmed by a broad verandah, and I loved to go in and see the little lamps shining so privately on opulent materials while all was so sunny and windy and fresh outside. She used to let me break open the wrappings of her overseas fashion magazines, which I think excited me first by their smell, that celebrated smell of the glossy mag, the scent of twentieth-century folly.

'Have any more come, Ida?' I would always ask.

She would not let me take them away, and as I knelt on the floor of her workroom and turned the pages, I was under enchantment again. What did they make me long for? Not the clothes, exactly. Nor the life shown, exactly.

'*I* don't know,' said Ida, when I asked her.

But Lewie Johns, kneeling on the floor by my side, moved one hand to and fro and said, 'Just to somehow approximate the style, that's all. I bet it's a chimera, though, all that style. In real life, when you got close to it, it would just melt away.'

Lewie was one of the artists. 'The worst of the lot,' he said, 'and *that's* saying something.' Honesty had made him give up all notions of painting and content himself with picking up a bit of commercial art here and there.

'And I'm not much chop at that, either.'

In times of idleness he would often come to Ida's rooms. 'Oh, I like *this*.' And he would walk about, draping himself in satin or lamé and striking poses that even now, in memory, surprise me by their wit. Sometimes the three of us would sit together and sew on a rush job, and at these times Lewie usually complained about his love affairs. Colin, my only mentor in these matters, had depicted homosexuality as something vile and horrendous, but by the time I thoroughly understood that the men Lewie complained about were not friends but lovers, it was too late to be horrified, because he had become the best friend I had had since my school days. With him I never played the game of exaggerating my shock. He had given me an early warning by breaking off his narrative, pointing a needle at me, and saying bitterly, 'Look at her face'. I soon became very artful at disguising my shock, although I must say here that as he became equally artful at detecting it, many sulks and squabbles were the result. But in spite of this we were (as Fred remarked long afterwards about the group at number six) 'hopelessly simpatico', and a dozen times a day I would think, 'I must show Lewie this', or 'I must tell Lewie that.' I had not acted on such fervent impulses of friendship since the time when Olive Partridge and I used to run across the paddocks to each other's houses with books we had just finished reading.

Every evening, at a quarter to six, Colin came home. He kissed me. 'And what did you do today?'

'I went over to Bomera.'

But one evening he frowned. 'I don't like that mob over there.'

'But Colin, you hardly know them.'

'I don't want to know them. If you ask me, they're pretty queer.'

'What's queer about Ida?'

'She seems a decent enough old stick. But most of the others look pretty queer.'

The word 'queer' had not then acquired its sexual shading. Colin used it simply in its original sense of 'unusual', but don't imagine it was much less hostile for that. The people at Bomera returned his dislike, and the manner in which they just barely refrained from expressing it, their sudden change, if I should mention his name, from frankness to cautious politeness, made it the more potently felt by me. None of them except Ida ever mentioned him first, and even Ida never spoke of him by name, but always called him 'him' or 'he'.

'You had better go now, Nora. He will be home soon.'

As time passed, and I also spoke of him as little as possible, the avoidance of his name became a conspiracy to which I consented so that I could enjoy their company while still persuading myself of love for Colin and my loyalty to him.

Ida Mayo was Lewie's chief confidante, but one day, when she was out, he came over to Crecy to complain about a man named Harold. I was cooking the dinner, and he stood behind me at the stove and talked. The difference in our heels made me hardly shorter than him that day, and presently, continuing to talk, he put his chin on my shoulder. It was the only time we ever touched each other.

Colin came in as he was leaving. After Lewie shut the door behind him, Colin continued to stand and stare at it, as if Lewie's image was imprinted there.

'You had that fellow in here? Alone?'

I was warned by his goggle eyes, his hollow tone of wonderment. 'Only for two or three minutes. He came to borrow some butter, but I don't see why we should lend him things.'

Colin was still staring at the door. 'Do you know what?'

'No. What?'

'I reckon he's a poofter.'

'Oh, Colin, he is not. He's engaged to a lovely girl in Adelaide. He showed me her photograph.'

'Anyone can have a *photo* of a girl.'

'Oh, but it had on the back of it, "To my darling Lewie, with all my love".'

'I don't care, I don't want him in here again.'

How quickly I became sly. After that, when Colin came home, and kissed me, and asked what I had done that day, I would say in an offhand way, 'Ah ... mm ... went and helped Ida for a bit. And, let's see ... what else? Goodness, I do hope I have a baby soon. I'm sick of not having enough to do. But never mind, it won't be for much longer.'

'It's been too long already. It's because you're frigid.'

'Perhaps it's you.'

'Perhaps. Only, I happen to know it isn't.'

'How?'

'I just happen to know, that's all.'

'But Colin, how?'

But Colin would say nothing more, and at that time I was afraid to encroach further on those silences of his, which I still hoped were charged with masculine mystery, and deep suggestion.

There comes back to me the smell of the downstairs hall of the city library. Was it malt? Or vinegar? But though I ascended so often in the wrought-iron cage, and though I sat so often reading in the deep window embrasures, I continued to discriminate in favour of the books lent to me by the artists at Bomera, first because they were crisp and fresh while those in the library were furred with use, and then because they had the approval of people I liked. The gentle watercolourist lent me his favourites: Saki, Chekhov, and Katherine Mansfield, and among the novels I borrowed from others were *Chrome Yellow*, *Sons and Lovers*, and *The Rainbow*. But it was from furred paper, in the old navy blue covers, that I read *Madame Bovary*.

The ignorance I still pretended of Colin now contended with a tide of theoretical knowledge. One day in the garden of Bomera, when we had been swimming, I watched two of the artists, a young man and woman, playing in the long grass below the timber walk of the pool. They were of a size, and both wore black wool costumes, and they rolled about like little bears, biting each other and laughing. I felt tears rising to my eyes. I had been married for more than two years. I left the pool and walked slowly through the garden to the house, past the rank shrubs, the dirty statues, and the summer-house with the stork on its peaked roof, dragging my towel behind me and hanging my head to hide my tears. I found Ida alone.

'Oh, Ida, why don't I have a baby?'

'Is *that* all you've got to cry about?'

'All!'

'Well, look, while you're waiting for this famous baby, why not take a job with me? I'll pay you well, and what's more, I'll teach you to *cut*. You've got original ideas, Nora, and your finish is lovely. But you can't *cut*.'

I said to Colin, 'Ida Mayo has offered me a job.'

'No wife of mine is going to work.'

'Colin won't let me,' I said to Ida.

'Oh, one of those.'

'It's his pride,' I said proudly.

'Is it? Well, I don't feel right about you helping me so often for nothing. He can't object if we make you a dress now and again. Or can he?'

'No,' said Colin, very slowly, 'that will be all right.'

Ida bought the materials and cut the dresses, and I made

them under her direction. I had begun to affect the gypsy sort of clothes the artists' girls wore, but as she fitted these new dresses on me Ida would say, 'Now, see how wrong you were about those arty things? These are your style.'

'Except for those clumpy shoes,' said Lewie.

'When he sees you in this dress,' said Ida, with pins in her mouth, 'he will want to buy you some new shoes.'

'I love these shoes,' I said.

Ida and Lewie said nothing. You could hear them saying it.

Every warm Saturday, Colin took me to the beach, every cool Saturday to the pictures, and every Sunday, whatever the weather, we went to see his mother and Les. We never saw Les's wife because on Sundays she took the children and went to see *her* mother, with whom Les had been feuding for eight years. It was feuding territory out there.

'Ooo,' said Una Porteous, 'another new frock.'

'All togged up again,' said Les.

'She got those dresses free, gratis, and for nothing,' said Colin.

'She'll have to let them out when the babies begin to come,' said Una Porteous.

'If they ever do,' said Les. 'Ha-ha-ha-ha-ha.'

Colin did not speak to me for four days. Then he reconciled himself to me in bed, and afterwards, I wept storms of tears.

'Oh, stop it,' he said wearily.

'It isn't as if I can help it.'

'Nobody's blaming you. I expect you'll fall one day.'

But I continued to weep because at last I had begun to admit the truth—that my greatest need was not for a baby. Indeed, there were times when I thought that all I wanted in the world was to be left alone in my beautiful room, close to people who never asked, audibly or otherwise, who I thought *I* was, but who nevertheless were interested in the answer to that question.

Then, suddenly, I was no longer frigid. I threw my arms about Colin. 'Oh, aren't you glad? Aren't you glad?'

'Yes, but I'm reading this.'

I felt that I wanted a baby after all. My night of wild tears seemed a temporary madness.

'Now we can have a baby,' I said.

'Yes, there's that.'

'God, you look lovely, Nora,' said the artists.

'My dear,' said the watercolourist sadly, 'you look as if a light has come on inside you.'

'God, you look healthy,' said Lewie with disgust.

'Ignore him, love,' said Ida.

Although I still thought, every day, 'I must show Lewie this,' or 'I must tell Lewie that,' I went less often to Bomera. I bought provisions at Kings Cross or in Macleay Street, and as I carried my basket home, under plane trees full of cicadas, I was proudly conscious of my status of housewife. I cut recipes from newspapers, and every night cooked as splendid a meal as our means would allow. I looked into prams, not with my former speculation, but with an expression of mindless doting, having cozened myself beforehand into liking what I saw. I told Colin that our baby would be a blond boy. I set my lips among the hairs on his sweating chest.

'I wanted to marry a dark man, but oh, I'm glad now I married a fair one.'

Empty cicada cases lay under the plane trees in Macleay Street. The trees shed their leaves, I read *Women in Love*, and Colin started to take me to football games. I stood with a hand tucked in the crook of his arm, while the cold entered my shoes, sent branches up my legs, and grew through my body like a tree of stone. I clung to his arm and was bewildered when he made an excited forward lunge and forgot that I was there. I was jealous of his absorption in the game, and estranged by the savagery of his shouting mouth. At home I was hurt when he read the newspaper at the dinner table, and I sulked when he took my arms from about his neck and absently put me to one side. I was unhappier than I had been before. My budget book, with its additions of halfpennies and pennies, threepences and sixpences, and its checked and disputed weekly balances, seemed to degrade my new and passionate love.

'An extra two-and-six? What for?'

'My shoes need mending.'

Colin examined one of them. 'They'll do for a while yet.'

And still, there was no baby.

'If you ask my opinion,' said Una Porteous, 'you're leaving it a bit on the late side.'

'I'll say!' said Les.

'A woman's figure has got to be ruined sooner or later,' said Una Porteous, 'no matter how good.'

I burst into tears.

'Unless,' cried Una in a powerful voice, 'you can't have any?'

'Boo-hoo!'

'Oh, sorry. If I had of known I would of cut my tongue out first. But I was not informed.'

Les spoke in a low but manly voice. 'I want you both to accept my sympathy.'

Colin looked out of the window.

'All the same,' said Una, 'what a tragedy for Col.'

'Can't be helped,' snapped Colin.

How clear all three of them looked through my tears—as clear and shining as fish in a fishmonger's streaming window.

Then, one day, I got a daring idea. I ran over to Bomera.

'Ida, I'll take that job.'

Ida dropped both hands to her lap. 'Oh, Nora, I offered it over a year ago. I'm not getting the work now. Haven't you noticed? It's this slump. People like me are the first affected.'

'Ida, I'm sorry.'

'Don't you worry about me, love. I'll get by. What's this about you? I thought he didn't want you to work.'

'I'm not asking him. I want to be independent.'

'Try the big places, I'll give you a reference.'

I tried the big places. 'Sorry,' they said, 'not just now.'

'Try the alteration rooms of the big stores,' said Ida.

But at the big stores they said, 'Nothing now. Perhaps later.'

Months went by. Whenever I quarrelled with Colin, I rushed out and tried the big places and the big stores. But now they both said the same thing.

'Not a hope. We're even putting people off.'

No new magazines were arriving at Ida's rooms, and Lewie made truth of fiction by coming over to Crecy to borrow butter. Sometimes he stayed for an hour or two, and we sat in a patch of sunlight on the floor, moving as it moved, and made up Ogden Nash verses. People no longer spoke of 'the slump', but of 'the Depression'. At last Lewie became so poor that he was forced to move to a very small room in Bayswater Road.

We sat at his window, looking out. 'So many people,' he said. 'And all those trams. Isn't it lovely?'

But I was sad. 'Do you ever feel like being a child again, Lewie?'

'Not if I had to go back to Wagga to be it.'

One day Colin came home from work looking pleased. 'Well,' he said, 'it's happened at last.'

'What?"

'Les is transferred to Forbes. We can go to Mum's.'

'What? But not to live?'

'And why not? Ah yes,' he said, looking into my face, 'I well remember you saying you would die if you had to live there. But we will see whether you die or not.'

'Of course I won't. I didn't mean *die*. But why must we go?'

'Nora, sit down.'

Because, whenever Colin wanted to talk to me 'seriously', we had to sit down. We sat down.

'Nora, haven't you heard of this Depression?'

'But you still have your job.'

'In the meantime.'

'You mean, you are threatened . . . ?'

'We are all threatened. For all I know, this week will be my last.'

'But even so, you have more than a thousand pounds in the bank.'

'So I'm to eat into my savings!'

'Is there no alternative to going out there?'

'I see none.'

'I do.'

'What?'

'Staying here.'

But Colin was giving me his stare of wonderment. 'Do you know something, Nora?'

'No. What?'

'You're mad.'

'I am not.'

'You are. I notice you haven't once considered Mum in all this. A widow. How is she going to get on without what Les kicked in for his keep?'

'But you always say Les is a bludg—'

'I'll do the swearing round here! He's a bludger, all right, but naturally, he had to kick in *some*thing.'

'Why can't she make the place into flats, and live in one of them?'

'Would you like to live in a flat, Nora, after having had your own home?'

'Yes.'

'Well, Mum's different.'

'I know. That's why I don't want to go.'

'Oh, come on, Nora, be reasonable. It won't be for long.'

'Oh. Won't it?'

'Of course not.'

'Why didn't you say so in the first place?'

'You didn't give me a chance.'

'How long?'

'Oh . . . just till we see how things work out.'

'Oh. And after that, could we come back here? Or some-where like it? Anyway, a place of our own?'

'I don't see why not. Come on, now—smile. *That's* better. Kissie, kissie, kissie.'

I went to Bomera and told the artists. 'Cheer up,' they said. 'It's not Timbuctoo. Half an hour in the train. You can come to see us often.'

I went and told Ida Mayo. She kissed me. 'Well, he's not the only one that's panicked. Come any time you like, Nora. I'm always here.'

I walked up to Bayswater Road and told Lewie. 'Jesus,' he said, 'you poor thing.'

'Oh, cheer up,' I said, 'it's not Timbuctoo. I'll come to town quite often.'

'Oh, good. And we can go for a walk, or to Ida's. And if we're terribly rich'—he raised his voice against the noise of a tram grinding up the hill to the Cross—'we can go for a *tram ride.*'

Very early the next day, Betty Cust comes to attend to my morn-ing needs and to make me a pot of tea, which she stays to share with me.

'Do you remember the Depression, Betty?' I have not slept well, and the question seems a natural extension of my night thoughts.

She replies that she remembers it very well. 'But it must

have been worse in the south, because such a lot of men came up here. Or perhaps that was because it's easier to be broke in a warm climate. They used to come to our place for hot water, or for tea or bread or anything else we could give them. Dad said we must have had a chalk mark on our gate, but I think it was only because we lived near the park. One afternoon I was coming home from school across the park, Nora, and a man suddenly sat up from where he had been lying in the long grass. Sat up and stared at me. And then lo and behold a woman sat up beside him. They were both still half asleep. They had been sleeping in the grass with their heads on rolls of blankets. Imagine in those days a woman humping a swag. There were hundreds of men, but that was the only time I saw a woman.'

'It wouldn't have occurred to most women then,' I say, 'though some must wish it had.'

'Not too awful, I suppose, as long as they could travel with a man for protection. Jack and I are going over to Clayfield this morning, Nora, with some plants for our daughter-in-law. But we'll be home in time for your lunch. And to get you up, I hope. Gordon Rainbow said he will try to get here about half past ten.'

'And he said I could get up?'

'He thinks so, for a while. Oh yes, and I brought you a pawpaw. I left it in the kitchen. It's not quite ripe yet.'

At about nine o'clock Lyn Wilmot comes.

'A pawpaw! They're not ripe here yet. It must have been sent down to them from Cairns. People are always sending the Custs things. Not that they need it. Oh well, to them that hath! That old newsagent's shop—you know that old newsagent's shop they had, with the great big backyard?'

'Yes. Somebody used to practise scales,' I say slowly, 'in the sitting room above the shop.'

'I wouldn't know. Long before my time. What I was going to say is, there's a supermarket there now. A hundred thousand,

the Custs are supposed to have got for the site. And just afterwards, Mrs Cust's mother died, and Mrs Cust got *her* place. And
what happened? Ampol bought it!'

But I am still hearing those piano scales, and am wonder-
ing why they give me a sense of uneasiness, even of danger. For
what can be dangerous about the Custs, the innocent Custs?
'Does Mr Cust play the piano?' I ask.

'Wouldn't have a clue. When are you going to be let up, by
the way?'

Her voice is sullen this morning, her manner incipiently
aggressive. Because she is tiring of her task, she is beginning to
bully me. I should be happy to be oblivious of such portents, but
after my term in Una Porteous's house, such innocence could
hardly be expected of me.

Lyn Wilmot moves slowly about the room, dusting and setting things straight.

'High time you were let up.'

'I hope it will be today.' And I add apologetically, 'I didn't
dream I would be so long in bed. If I had, I would have gone to
a hospital.'

'*He* should have known. Doctor Smith would have known. I
wouldn't have Doctor Rainbow if you paid me. Doctor Smith's
good. We've had Doctor Smith ever since we've been here.'

I try to deflect her anger. 'And how long is that, Mrs Wilmot?'

'Best part of three years.'

'Then you would hardly have had a chance to know my
sister.'

'Not to know her, no. She wasn't easy to know, was she? I got
on all right with her, what I saw of her, but Gary and her had a
big row about her mango tree shading our vegetable bed. That
big mango out the back.'

'So the old mango tree is still there!'

'I'll say it's still there! Not that it's any good to anyone. It's the old sort with fibrous fruit. But never mind—she wouldn't have parted with that mango tree for one million dollars.'

Again I am reminded of Una Porteous, who also liked to use the figure of one million for emphasis. 'I would not see husband and wife unhappy,' she used to say, 'for one million pounds.'

Or happy, I used to think, for two million.

Lyn Wilmot's resemblance to Una Porteous is becoming more remarkable by the minute. Again she is dusting with her husband's worn singlet, and after shaking it out of the window, she stays there for a while, looking up and down the street with the same strange aimless longing with which Una Porteous used to look up and down the street from her front door. That, if anything could have, might have reconciled me to Una Porteous.

But when Lyn Wilmot turns into the room again, she resumes her dusting in a manner more slouching and sullen than ever.

'Wouldn't you think that with all his money your nephew would have had you live down there with him, instead of up here all alone?'

I open the drawer of my bedside table and write on my shopping list, 'yellow duster'. Then I close the drawer and say, 'I loathe living in other people's houses, Mrs Wilmot. I loathe it.'

'Yes, but when you think of it, when it comes down to tin tacks, if it wasn't for the Custs having nothing to do with their time ... what I mean to say is, it's okay living alone as long as you're not a burden on others.'

Also like Una Porteous, she disowns her arrow as soon as it reaches its mark. 'Not that I mean anything by that! Oh, I hope you don't think I *mean* ...'

I interrupt these protestations. 'Of course you didn't, my dear.'

'Oh, I could cut out my tongue.'

.

It is really too bad that I should be afflicted with this reincarnation of Una Porteous. But I smile, and beg her not to cut out her tongue. I turn the conversation to enquire about her two little girls. I ask their names and ages, and express interest in their schooling.

'And are they as pretty as you?' I ask at last.

'I don't know about pretty. They're all right, I suppose.'

But her grudging tone cannot conceal her pleasure. She flicks her husband's singlet about at a great rate. 'I'll just run down and bring up your newspaper before I go. Mrs Cust must've forgotten it. Now there's nothing else you want? *Sure?*'

I suppose that is how I ought to have treated Una Porteous from the start, but in those days I should have been ashamed, for her as well as for myself, if I had employed such crude tactics. And so, instead of lashing out with flattery when cornered, I allowed my feelings to show, in one way or another, and by the time I had learned the defensive uses of flattery, and had deteriorated enough to enjoy the private revenge to be gained from watching it work, it was too late to heal the breach made by my initial frankness, although not too late to spread a smear of false goodwill over my relations with her. Coarse fighting would have been healthier, but I doubt if I could have kept it up for all the time I lived in her house.

Five years. Five years of waste, and worse than waste, and all unnecessary. In that famous Depression there were pockets of prosperity. Colin never lost his job, though he constantly said (and perhaps believed) that 'for all he knew, this week would be his last.' It was winter when we went there, and outside the window of the bedroom assigned to us stood a lemon tree heavy with fruit. I took fire from the yellow and green and asked Colin if I might make new curtains and a bedcover. I explained that when we got our own place, I would adapt them, and since both bed and windows were bare, he had to agree.

'Better get good stout stuff though,' he said.

I rang Lewie and told him I was coming into town, and after buying the good stout stuff I met him on Farmer's corner. It was only a fortnight since I had seen him, and I was shocked by the change in him, his look of poverty and illness.

'Thank God for the bourgeoisie!' he said when he saw me.

That night I gave the bill for the material to Colin. In the train on the way home, I had had a revulsion against pretending to lose the change, and had determined to tell the truth, and face it out.

'I lent the change to Lewie Johns,' I said.

'You what?'

'He was hungry.'

'How do you know he was hungry?'

'He told me so when I met him.'

'Ah,' said Colin. Colin never lost his temper. 'So you met him?'

'Yes.'

'By appointment?'

'Yes.'

'And you gave him, let me see,' said Colin, consulting the bill, 'you gave him one pound, three and sixpence, of my money.'

'Yes.'

'Right!' said Colin.

I dared not challenge his ominous composure. He was the only other inhabitant of my domain. I made white curtains and a yellow bedcover, and varnished the floor black. I was fortunate in the unpapered walls—all I had to do was kalsomine them white—and as for the massive hideous wardrobe and dressing table, I simply determined not to look at that side of the room any more than I could help. Una Porteous offered me a mat with roses on it, but I, too fired by my scheme for tact, cried no, no, no, I would make a hooked one. 'Who does she think *she* is?'

Her bridling shoulders said it as she turned away. In retrospect I can understand her offence, but at the time I hardly noticed. I polished the brass bedstead and painted a honey jar white and filled it with flowers from the garden. And I was delighted, when I had finished, because I had made it from so little.

'It is hard and unfemin-*ine*, if you ask me,' said Una Porteous.

'It's all right,' said Colin.

My half room and my husband became my only pleasures. Lying under the yellow bedcover, I would watch Colin undress, and as he was getting into bed I would reach out, and pull him down towards me, and sigh with relief at the contact. One night he said quietly that not every man liked his wife to behave like a whore, and a few weeks later he cried in spontaneous anger, 'Look, just lie still, will you? That's all you have to do.'

Whether my submissiveness is ingrained or was implanted I do not know. I only know that all open aggression on my part, in whatever field, has always led me to sorrow and retreat. But beneath my renewed submission a sour rebellion lay. I was told that there was no money for fares to the city. 'We can think ourselves lucky,' said Colin, 'to have a roof over our heads, and food to eat.'

'And besides,' said Una, 'when our local shops are having such a thin time, it's them we should deal off, and not go traipsing into town all the time.'

I didn't have a penny. I would certainly have tried to fiddle the housekeeping money, only, Colin now gave it to Una Porteous.

'It's Mum's house, after all.'

'Yes, and I am sure Nora wouldn't begrudge me handling the money in my own home.'

I asked for a small allowance, and Colin said he would think about it. A fortnight later I asked if he had thought about it.

'Thought about what?' he said to his shaving mirror.

'My allowance.'

'What allowance?'

'You must remember.'

'Must I?' He was inclined to be humorous. 'Well, I don't.'

I went back to the beginning and made my request again. When I had finished he pulled his mouth awry to tauten the skin under the blade. A minute passed in silence except for the scrape of the razor. Then he leaned forward and looked intently into his own eyes.

'But why bring that up when I am shaving?'

He was shaving, he was reading the newspaper, he was just about to turn on the wireless, he had to go out and mow the lawn, he must get his eight hours sleep.

'Then when *can* we discuss it?' I cried at last.

'One day soon, don't worry.'

But when I asked again, 'one day soon', he sighed heavily, folded his arms, and raised his eyes to the ceiling. In that attitude, he heard me out, and then rose and left the room without a word in reply. I lost my head, and followed him, and threw myself against his silence, railing.

'If you'll excuse me saying so,' said Una Porteous, 'you don't know how to *handle* a man.'

Unable to entreat any longer without utter abasement, I stopped. And a little later, when I mentioned moving to a place of our own, and Colin replied with surprise, 'But why should we move? We're quite comfortable here,' I knew it was the reply I had inwardly expected, and that I must speak of moving no more.

Ever since my marriage, in my letters to my mother and Grace, pride had made me pretend to a perfect tranquility, but one day, while writing to my mother, my guard crashed down and I let pour forth on the paper a long and passionate complaint. It was Grace who replied, with an exhortation to duty, unselfishness, and common sense. She remarked how strange it was that Colin, about whose virtues I was always boasting, had developed these dreadful characteristics 'all of a sudden'. She felt she was sure that now I had had time to cool down I would be seeing things once more in their proper perspective. She said that she was 'a great believer in working with the material to hand . . .

'. . . and not crying for the moon, which has always been your big drawback, Nora.'

She then gave a page of trifling news items, and ended with a request not to write any more letters like that, 'because they worry poor mother'.

I tore her letter into tiny pieces, flushed them down the lavatory, and ran from the house. I went to the local shops, one by one, and asked for work. Of the people I asked, I remember nothing but their refusals. Only for the newsagent's wife. I can still see her angry face as she replied.

'You've got a nerve, Mrs Porteous. Thousands out of work, men hungry, yet here you are asking for work. You with a husband to keep you!'

I walked to the next suburb, where nobody knew me, and went from shop to shop. I would have done anything, but nobody wanted anything done. In my beautiful dress, I walked the streets like an invisible person. I went home and wrote to Lewie.

What causes exiles the most distress
Is that nobody recognizes their national dress.

It was returned a week later, marked *Address Unknown*. I rang Ida.

'I can't say where he is, love. All I know is, he's done a bunk. I think he owed so many bits of money, here and there, that in the end it embarrassed him to see people. Even me, though I told him and told him.'

My few books, all poetry, became useless to me. My panicky mind blocked the rhythms and garbled the words, and very soon I began to wonder what I had ever seen in them. The only other books in the house were school texts, and the nearest free library was my old haunt in the city. A neighbour lent me *The Forsyte Saga*, and I still associate it so firmly with that period of my life that even the names of the characters depress me. I refused to watch it on television with Hilda and Liza and Fred.

'Say Soames,' said Liza, 'and she screams.'

But in spite of the comedy I made of my marriage for my friends at number six, I see now how extremely selective I was, and how many incidents and areas of feeling I did not touch upon, or could not have touched upon, because I had forgotten them until now. I had forgotten how increasingly sly I became. Outwardly calm now, and ingratiating, I would await the opportunity to steal threepences and sixpences from Una's purse or Colin's trousers.

Fred loved Elizabethan prose, and often quoted from it. The words I am thinking of went something like this, '*Want cannot be withstood. A man can do but what he can do, and when the lion's skin is out at the elbows, why then, the fox's case must help.*'

My lion's skin, never too sound from the start, must have been out at the elbows indeed for me to adopt so readily the skin of the fox. The image of myself as sneak thief comes back the more vividly for having lain so long quiescent. There I stand, one hand cupping purse or pocket to control the chink of coins, while the other dips, and selects by touch. My eyes are turned towards the door, my heart beats light and fast, and my ears strain to gauge my safety by the two voices in the living room. The coin pinched and pocketed, I prance on tip-toe to the lavatory, where I pull the chain before loudly opening and shutting the door. I then saunter back to the living room, where Una Porteous has just turned on the wireless. Three chairs are grouped about the cabinet. Meek in my revenge, ascendent in my secrecy, I fold my hands, and sit, and smile.

One curious sidelight occurs to me here. At that time there was a newspaper in Sydney called *Smith's Weekly*, a coarse-grained affair of cartoons and 'humorous' articles. One of its regular themes concerned wives stealing from their husbands' pockets. The popular acceptance of these jokes suggests that in Australia I had many sisters in petty theft. But perhaps such jokes were also current elsewhere in the world at that time. I have no means of knowing.

I secreted all I stole, and when I had enough, I went to see Ida Mayo, being careful to choose those days when Una Porteous visited a cousin in a distant suburb. At Bomera the big double doors still stood open, Folly and Wisdom still faced each other across the marble hall, and in Ida's rooms the little lamps still shone, though on less opulent and fewer materials. There was a new lot of artists, shabbier than the last, but outwardly just as insouciant.

'They do help each other out,' said Ida. 'I'll say that much for them.'

'No word from Lewie?' I would ask.

'I did hear he was in Melbourne. Things aren't quite as bad there. New South Wales is the worst hit. Still, I'm getting by. These slumps don't last for ever. Just hang on, Nora, and I'll give you that job after all. And in the meantime, keep your hand in.'

Sometimes the gentle watercolourist would be sitting in Ida's rooms. 'That's right, sweetheart, whatever work you do, always keep your hand in.'

To keep my hand in, I made dresses for Una Porteous and her friends. I had never made a garment for anyone but myself, and at first I was dismayed by my lack of skill in cutting the cloth so that I was able to construct it round these variously shaped bodies, but they praised me so lavishly and repeatedly that my critical sense gradually diminished, and my standards were undermined. I read Colin's school books and became fascinated by geometry. I worked through the first theorems and at night deserted the wireless to sit in our bedroom and solve problems. Una Porteous took my chair from the group of three and set it in ostentatious loneliness against a wall. I was thirty. 'You would never think it,' said the women for whom I made dresses. And they were right. When I caught sight of my reflected face I was startled to see it still so fair and candid. I discarded Colin's geometry book, seized his French grammar instead, and found it much to my liking. My mutterings irritated Una Porteous.

'But what good will it do you?'

I would raise my face and give her a preoccupied smile. '*Ai-je? As-tu? A-t-il? A-t-elle?*'

Helped by the memory of my own school French, I made good progress, except, of course, for my grotesque pronunciation. I began to defend myself with French verbs. When I was furious with Colin I no longer lost my temper, but said with smiling vehemence into his face, '*Fus, fus, fut, fûmes, fûtes, furent.*'

I was thirty-one, thirty-two. Panic attacked me again, the strong bird rising. I began to walk again.

The pattern I traced this time with my feet, dictated by streets and houses, was rectilinear, and as I walked I looked into the faces of passers-by, and hoped for rescue in fantastic ways. I was thirty-three. I sometimes rang Ida, but no longer went to see her. Deterred by an obscure shame, I no longer left the suburb. I had good food, the necessary clothes, a fire against the cold, a dentist to maintain my teeth, and a doctor to attend me in illness. Newspapers and magazines came into the house,

Una Porteous would furnish me with writing paper and stamps on request, and for all other needs I made application to Colin. To explain my growing fear of leaving the suburb, I told myself that I was waiting for ideal conditions. I now used my stolen money to buy lottery tickets in false names. On buying the ticket I would be filled with light-heartedness and a belief that I would, must, win, and at this stage I studied the "To Let" columns of the *Herald* and made detailed and continuously changing lists of the books and clothes I would buy. Trust would then decline to a mere fervent hope, and during this stage I memorized the number of the ticket and whispered it over and over on my walks. But on the morning of the drawing I always lost all hope, and when the results were published I read them impassively, without disappointment.

On my walks, because I never saw any other walker as regular as myself, my thoughts sometimes turned to Dorothy Irey. This was the time when Grace's and my mother's letters were telling me of her clever children, her good husband who was 'doing so well,' and the extended house that Grace said was 'the best home in the street'. As I walked I would imagine myself in her place, but would feel neither regret nor envy, because I knew that I did not want that either. Married to Bruce Rainbow, and living in 'the best home in the street', I knew I would still have been mad with restlessness, and moreover would have had the guilt of having become the plague of a kindly man.

'All very well for her,' I would tell myself. 'She's so gentle. But I'm not.'

At that time I also thought a great deal of Olive Partridge. Grace's tantalizing news of Olive was that she had written a novel. '*One of those modern things. I can't say I cared for it much.*' I knew the name of it—*Cut and Choose*—but I had neither seen nor read it. My correspondence with Olive had become thin, and had then petered out. Recently I had made several attempts to write to her, but the banality that was the curse of my letters to my family now extended to my attempts to write to Olive.

And only now, back in Queensland, in my late seventies, do I suddenly understand why. I was banal because I was lying. If my pride had allowed me to tell the truth, my letters would not have been banal.

The cut in Colin's salary was well compensated by the drop in prices. He enrolled us both in the Green Gardens Tennis Club and bought me a racquet, canvas shoes, and the stuff for a pleated dress. I still felt the heat terribly, and in the early afternoons I sat inertly in the tennis shed, going into a doze in which the percussion of balls grew louder and louder in my head until it startled me awake. But when the shadows lengthened across the court, and I felt the stirring of cool air on my bare arms, I would jump to my feet and wait impatiently for my turn to play.

The vehemence of my game embarrassed Colin. 'Tone it *down*,' he whispered.

All the wives brought cakes or scones to the Green Gardens Tennis Club.

'They really liked that cake of yours,' Colin would say, in a satisfied voice, on the way home.

'I liked Molly Furlong's cake.'

'Not a patch on yours. They really liked that cake of yours.'

Compliments on my youthful appearance pleased him less. When the local 'sheik' said, 'I could fall for your wife, Col, I really could', I would feel Colin's eyes upon me in a sharp and hostile appraisal that belied his laughing mouth, and that night, without speech or preamble, he would seize me and fling himself upon me in methodical but frenzied sexual labour, while I maintained my detachment by murmuring inwardly, '*Que tu sois, qu'il soit, que nous soyons . . .*' For on those occasions when my blood rose, and I could not help but respond, I considered myself vanquished, and felt humiliated beyond endurance. Far more than Colin's person, I had grown to hate the physical bond between us, and the moment when we got into bed, and lay down side by side, was for me a moment of intense and bitter misery.

In my plans for escape I included no lover, but in my hours of lonely sewing and musing, when my head was bent over my work, and the crow of the backyard rooster rose above the distant hubbub of the primary school, I would become conscious of a heart-swelling hope, a vibrant space at my left side, a yearning in the nerves of my skin. Never once did I allow these longings to take on the density of an ideal, as I would formerly have done, but nor did I try to extinguish them. I kept them, rather, at a delicate distance.

Employers were advertising in the *Herald* once more. Junior Shop Assistant. Expert Shorthand-typiste. Experienced Tailoress. They could still afford to take their pick. I had quite stopped telephoning Ida. On Saturday nights, Colin, with his legs crossed and one foot jigging, sat between his mother and me at the local picture theatre. He bought a Dodge motor car, and every Sunday morning he cleaned and polished it on the driveway near the front gate. I think the closest I ever came to attacking him physically was one Sunday afternoon, when, as I got into the front seat beside him, he said in one of his genial outbursts, 'Well, Mrs Porteous, aren't you proud of your nice clean car?' On most Sunday afternoons, he would take Una Porteous and me to visit those of his relatives who had not suffered too badly in the Depression. The men collected round 'the Dodge', while I sat with the soporific women. In this society, where there were no 'sheiks', they said I was artistic and refined, but had no sense of humour. 'Nora's a bit like Bette Davis,' someone would occasionally remark. But Bette Davis was nobody's favourite actress.

These relations, and the tennis people, because they were shared acquaintances, did siphon off some of the tension caused by the co-habitation of bitter enemies. Their conception of our marriage presented us with a model by which, if we pretended to follow it, we could avoid total disaster. Thus passed many months of meaningless harmony, slick as a ribbon but studded with carbuncles of silent misery. Who was I? Nora Porteous, née Roche, thirty-five, domestic worker, amateur dressmaker, detested concubine, and student of the French subjunctive tense.

'Why don't you charge for those dresses you make?' asked Colin one day.

'I thought you didn't want me to.'

'Times have changed.'

I had so settled into our uneasy jogtrot that it took me some time to realize that Colin had also changed. For years only the compliments and criticisms of others had made him notice me, but now, as if he had stepped over an invisible line, he began to circle me and rake me with his eyes.

'Your legs are getting thin. Why are your legs getting so thin?'

He reached out and ran a finger along my jaw line. 'That's where you'll go first, when you start to go. When you bend your head you're puffy just there.' I would wake to find that he had turned his head on the pillow and was staring at me with hatred, and I would turn away or leap out of bed. At the table I would bend over my plate to escape the same brooding stare. It was an invasion. My enemy had entered my hut and was squatting in a corner, waiting. Now, when I was alone and sewing, I was no longer visited by longings for love, but by dread that attacked me like an unhealthy mist. When I went into the bathroom, and a moth flew into my face, I screamed and sobbed. One day I embarked on a walk but at the first corner turned suddenly and made for home at an ugly panicky trot. I grew thin and silent, and as I knelt at the feet of the women, with pins in my mouth, I was conscious that their commonplace words held undertones of pity and curiosity.

Una Porteous walked about the house heaving sad gusty sighs. 'If only you had learned how to *handle* him!'

The depression was over. The women were happy to pay me for making their dresses. At best, I could have left entirely, and at the worst could have sought alleviation in change. I did neither. I excused my terror of leaving the house by telling myself that I must not waste time and money on the mere alleviation of my state, but must stay in the meantime, and work, and save for total freedom.

Three months after I had begun to earn money, Colin came home with a girl.

'This is Pearl,' he said.

Pearl burst into tears and ran to the window and stood with her back to the room. I looked at her back, observed with distant accuracy the set of her raglan sleeves, and then turned to Colin. His eyes were waiting for me, and the hatred that had brooded there so long now flared out clear and victorious.

'I want a divorce,' he said. 'I want to marry Pearl. I'll do the right thing about money, of course. And then, there's your dressmaking.'

My voice, when it came, was thin and meek and choked.

'All right.'

But then anger struck like a gust from outside me, making me dizzy. I can hear my voice now, loud with spite.

'I hope she will be able to *handle* you!'

Pearl turned from the window. 'I'll tell you one thing I won't do,' she cried through her tears.

I was taking the opportunity thoroughly to inspect her, so I suppose I sounded preoccupied. 'What won't you do?'

'I won't take Col's hard-earned money,' she wailed, 'and give it to queenie boys.'

'Where are they playing tennis, Doctor Rainbow?'

He has just arrived, and has put a thermometer under my arm. 'What do you mean?'

'I woke up hearing it. Can't you hear it?'

'No, I can't.'

'I often hear it. The first time I thought it was a dream, but this time I'm sure. Listen. There it is again.'

'Oh,' he says, 'that. That's shooting from the rifle range. Miles away, but this northerly brings it.'

'It sounds exactly like tennis.'

'I shouldn't have thought so.' He is looking at me keenly. 'Does it disturb you?'

'I find it melancholy.'

'I'll shut the window.'

'Most of us,' he remarks quietly, as he comes back after shutting the window, 'have some sound that disturbs us.'

'Do you?'

He hesitates. 'I don't like wind in trees. I think that's a fairly common dislike.'

'I like it. When my nephew was young I used to take him to catch yabbies in the creek. There were she-oaks close by, and the sound of the wind in them was so peaceful, I've always remembered it. Is that deep little creek still there? Behind the school?'

'I don't know,' he says. 'We'll have that thermometer now.'

He reads the thermometer, puts it back in its case, then turns away to shut his bag. 'You can't get up today.'

'What?'

'I'm sorry. Except to go to the toilet, perhaps with somebody's help.'

'I understood from Betty Cust . . .'

'That was dependent on how you were.'

'I am quite well.'

'You'll be even better tomorrow.'

'Very well, Doctor Rainbow.'

Does he detect the challenge in this evident agreement? He gives me one of his quick looks. I meet his eyes and penetrate for the first time the barrier of his forbidding appearance and see something gentle and friendly and humble in his regard that reminds me of Dorothy. I open my mouth to remark on the resemblance, then recall that I am forbidden the subject, and at the same time a possible reason for the embargo occurs to me.

Did Dorothy commit suicide, and did he, perhaps, find her?

No sooner have I formed the question than I realize it has been lying just beneath the surface of my consciousness, waiting to be asked.

I get up as soon as he goes. Very slowly, with one hand against the wall, I make my way to the bathroom, and although I am trembling when I get back into bed, I feel none the worse for it. When Betty comes to get my lunch I tell her that I am mortified beyond endurance by chamber pots and dependence, and that it will not be necessary for Lyn Wilmot to do anything more for me.

But Betty's calm smile makes me feel I am making a big silly fuss over nothing. 'Oh, let her keep on, Nora. You're getting well so quickly now.'

'I don't want her. A bit of dust won't hurt, and everything else I can manage for myself.'

'You're being stubborn. Do you want to undo all our good work? Do you?'

'Oh, very well,' I say with a cross sigh.

She laughs. 'Sometimes you remind me of Grace.'

'I have just been thinking of Grace. Was she very much distressed when Dorothy died?'

I intend this as an introduction to my question. 'It made a very great difference to Grace,' says Betty. But she speaks warily, and hurries away to the kitchen, and I am so touched by her concern for me, and so amused by her innocence in believing me to be vulnerable and tender-hearted—*me!*—that I desist from the question, and decide to let her tell me in her own way, in her own time. She makes my lunch, and after she has cleared away the things she comes and stands by the foot of my bed, looking pleased with herself and hiding something behind her back.

'A surprise, Nora. Put your glasses on.'

I reach for my spectacles, 'Letters!'

The pleasure leaves her face. 'No. I raised your hopes. I'm sorry.'

'I thought the mail strike may be over.'

'No. I wish it were. It's only this. Although,' she says as she brings it from behind her back, 'I mustn't say *only* this.'

She holds it up, an embroidered wall hanging. 'The one you made for mother. I told you I would bring it.'

I raise my eyebrows and stare, so astonished by the excellence of the design and the beauty of the colour that I cannot speak. Betty is delighted by my response. Laughing, she brings the tapestry to me and spreads it over my knees.

'How you had the patience!' she says.

I examine the back of it. 'It must have been a fluke.'

'If that's what you think, I'll get hold of some of the others. Old Mrs Partridge's. And I'll ask Gordon Rainbow to bring the one you made for Dorothy.'

I turn the embroidery to the right side and run the flat of my hand over it. 'An orange tree,' I say. And I hear myself, during those first few northern winters, telling people that I was going home, and that never again would I live in a climate where oranges don't grow. 'Do you mind if I keep this for a while?' I ask Betty.

'As long as you like.'

I put it out of sight on the lower shelf of my beside table, but for the rest of Betty's visit my consciousness of it makes me absentminded, and as soon as she goes I snatch it up and examine it by the light of the reading lamp.

I am pleased to find many little flaws in it, and moreover in this case it would have been better if I had combined a little wool with my silks. But these criticisms made, I am forced to return to my first estimate of its merit. The leaves and fruit of the orange tree compose a tight bouquet above a straight trunk, and eight little birds, all fabulous yet touchingly domestic, strut or peck beneath it. They are in danger of giving it a spotty effect, and yet they don't, and that risk, taken and surmounted, is its merit and distinction. Alternately I grieve for that lost time, and rejoice that it was not lost entirely. Much of my long life can be apportioned into periods of waiting, but during that first long period perhaps I was able to play and create because for most of the time I waited *without panic*, whereas in the second long period, in the iron-grey and terracotta suburb, all my little talents were blighted by panic and despair, so that there were only the ill-cut dresses for the women, and the cakes for the tennis club.

Colin offered me a settlement of three hundred pounds, in return for which I was to leave him and allow him to divorce me for desertion. I would have accepted gratefully if it had not been for Colin's own lawyer. He was one of the men at the tennis club. He had a local office, and having seen Una Porteous pass his windows, he took the opportunity of ringing me privately.

'Your husband has told me a great deal about your faults. Too much. But one thing he didn't mention was your stupidity. You are entitled to much, much more than three hundred pounds.'

'Am I? Why?'

I heard him sigh. 'Because the law says so. You know what I'm doing, don't you, talking to you like this?'

'What, ethics or something?'

At the tennis club he used to slap his forehead in exasperation at his own play. I think he did it now. 'Or something! You are legally entitled,' he continued flatly, 'to an income for life. He wants the divorce, not you.'

'Oh no, you're mistaken. I want it too.'

'You didn't instigate it.'

'I would have, sooner or later.'

'Irrelevant. You didn't.'

'I intended to leave him.'

'Irrelevant. You didn't.'

'Three hundred is all I want. It's a matter of pride.'

I think he hit himself on the forehead again. 'Pride!'

'All I want is a stake until I can earn a living.'

'But can you earn a living? You're untrained. Times aren't easy yet. And you're no longer young.'

'I'm only thirty-five.'

But as I said the words, it sounded old, and I was filled with panic, and a longing for the undemanding dullness and steady misery of my captivity. His persuasive speech continued, and I looked at my lap, and heard only noise and garbled words, until he raised his voice and said angrily, 'At the very least, the *very least*, you must ask for a thousand pounds.'

I lifted my head. A thousand! I was thunderstruck at the thought of all that money. I was tempted, assailed by longings for pleasure, books, silk stockings, a room of my own, a hat like Mary Astor's. I felt strong and brave again, with not a scruple left. 'All right!' I cried. 'I will!'

A week of wrangling and indignation followed.

'A thousand! Poor boy!'

'A bloody thousand, no less!'

'Skinning the poor boy out!'

'Talk about gold diggers!'

But I, silent, determined, and perfectly composed, met all lesser offers by shaking my head and giving a slow smile. Until, in a ten-second turnabout, I settled for less.

'Okay, okay—eight hundred.'

I was packing my suitcase as I spoke—or shouted, rather—at the top of my voice. They brought me a statement to sign. I signed it and pushed it violently away. Una Porteous came to say a sweet and tragic goodbye, but I pushed her away too. I believe now that that frenzy of movement and shouting, that blind rush, was an instinct on my part to build up a momentum on which I could forget my terror of leaving the house, but at the time, even as I went on like that, a detached part of me was standing by and making comment.

'Oh, look at you, going on like this. You're certainly mad. Is that you shouting? Yes, it is. Goodness.'

Anyway, my ruse, if it was that, worked, and two hours later I was lying upside down on a narrow bed at the Menzies Hotel in Elizabeth Street, with my eyes shut, my hands folded behind my head, and my feet crossed on the bedhead. I assured myself that I was calm and steady, but I know now that I was neither. I had the money saved from my dressmaking (twenty-eight pounds) and Colin's cheque for eight hundred. After an hour I got up and made myself go out. It was a miracle. In those crowded streets, where nobody knew who I was, my trepidation was absorbed as easily as the sound of my footsteps, which in the streets of the suburb had sounded so loud and outrageous. I went to David Jones and bought four novels and a handkerchief of fine white linen with a broad yellow border.

Of the people I had known at Bomera, only Ida and the gentle watercolourist were left. The remittance men looked like confidence men, Folly and Wisdom had their toenails painted red and cigarette bumpers stuck in their mouths, and the current lot of artists and their girls were so drunken, broke, gay, and anarchic that they made the first lot appear, by contrast, mere decorous fancy-dress Bohemians.

Ascending the staircase I encountered a group of them descending, and they surrounded me to comment first on my hat ('Robin Hood or Pinocchio?'), and then on my hair, which I had had cropped to a bob that morning.

'If you look at the underside of the cut,' said a man named Wallace Faulks 'you can see the grain. Look, just like in a section of wood.'

I was charmed by such detailed observation, which reminded me of Lewie. It was as a guest (always rather detached) at one of their parties that I happened to hear Daff tell the story of the abortion car.

I suppose her name was Daphne, but I never heard her called anything but Daff. The big black car left, she said, every Monday and Wednesday and sometimes Thursday, from Doctor So-and-so's rooms in Macquarie Street, opposite the Botanical Gardens. It collected 'that day's batch', and after leaving the Gardens passed Parliament House, Sydney Hospital, the Old Mint, and then took the curve out of Macquarie Street to go past the Registry of Births, Deaths and Marriages and St Mary's Cathedral before turning sharply at the Blind Society Building to head for the eastern suburbs.

I wondered why everybody was laughing. I couldn't see the joke until Daff said that she had asked the driver if he couldn't make a little detour and pass Darlinghurst Gaol. 'He wasn't a bit amused', said Daff. I saw the point then.

But in spite of my interest in the company of the artists and their girls, my detachment from them grew. Some were only eighteen, none more than twenty-five. They made me feel the full dull weight of those wasted years.

'They all drink such a lot,' I complained to Ida.

'Don't they! Even those nice young actors.'

'It would be good to see Lewie again.'

'I still haven't a notion where he's got to. And anyway, he'll have changed too.' Ida flung out both hands. 'Everything's changed. It changed everything.'

Prosperity had not returned to Ida. 'I'm making enough to live on, and please God, I always will. But those plans I had for expansion—a good little shop with a workroom—you know the way we used to talk?—all that's had to go by the board. I'm sixty-three, and last year I had a bit of heart trouble.'

Among the books I had bought on the day of my release were both Olive Partridge's novels, the second one a very recent publication. Lying on my bed at Menzies Hotel, I read them with growing puzzlement, because I could find no trace in them of the Olive I had known. In the course of reading she gradually altered in my mind until she became a tall, beautiful, 'troubled' woman in a long green dress that moved about her 'like water'. I knew perfectly that this was a composite image of several of her characters, but all the same, from that time, until I met Olive again, every time I thought of her, that is what I saw.

I stayed at Menzies for two weeks. I read, I bought clothes, I visited at Bomera. In the Botanical Gardens I walked along narrow paths and let one hand lag idly on foliage. And more and more often, without warning, I would feel the same surge of excitement and strength as when Colin's lawyer had said, 'One thousand pounds.' Where there had been a vibrant space at my side, there was now an intimation of a presence, and sometimes, in a silent greenhouse or palm grove, I nearly turned towards it, whispering.

'You're looking better every day,' said Ida.

I went to her mirror and looked at my face as if it were somebody else's. 'It's almost puzzling, how the body recovers.'

'It's hope that does it.'

'I hope for nothing,' I said, in the laconic way that was becoming my habit.

The watercolourist, an old man now, spent much of his time in Ida's rooms, and I would often interrupt their little treats for two, buttered crumpets, welsh rarebit, or chicken soup, over which they were as absorbed as children.

'You will soon be getting married,' I told Ida one day.

'He's a dear old fellow, but I'll marry nobody.'

'Neither shall I.'

'You? *You* will. What else can you do?'

'What a thing to say! Work, of course.'

'What at?'

'Oh, something.' Through the French doors of Ida's room, beyond the verandah, I could see a ship coming in to berth. 'But first of all,' I heard myself saying, 'I'm going away.'

'Where to?'

I didn't really have a firm intention of going anywhere, but I said London because it was the first place I thought of. And to myself I said that I could go, too, if I pleased. Nobody could stop me. I jumped to my feet and laughed. 'Yes,' I said, 'that's where I'm going. London.'

And that's how I came to go to London, not because I particularly wanted to, but as an affirmation of the wonderful discovery that *nobody could stop me*.

'Nora,' said Ida, 'that eight hundred won't last for ever. And if you truly don't want to remarry, what will you do when it's gone? You're too old for shop jobs. They won't pay senior wages to inexperienced women. And when it comes right down to the honest truth, you're still only an amateur dressmaker. You still can't *cut*.'

I laughed. 'You and your cutting! I'll be back in a year, and I'll still have some money. Time enough to think about it then.'

When I went to book my passage I discovered that somebody *could* stop me. Colin. We were not yet divorced, and my 'husband' must give signed permission for me to go. He gave it, of course. What better evidence of desertion than a wife who went tripping, traipsing, gallivanting overseas?

While Ida was making my travelling clothes I went north to see my mother and Grace. It was an uncomfortable visit. Some families have an almost uncanny power of forcing an alienated member to behave according to its opinion of him or her, and as soon as I divined, in their reserved greetings, their questions, and their set reproachful mouths, the discussions they had had about me, I began to act in a manner to confirm them in their opinion. In Ida's rooms I could bow my head and tell my woes, but at my mother's table all I could do was to sit upright and make smart cracks about marriage and divorce. She and Grace would have been ready to console me for being broken and rejected, but could not forgive me for my apparent gaiety, for wearing the first trousers they had ever seen 'in the street', or for painting my toenails pink. Reckless. Cynical. Frivolous. Those were the words they used about me. And rebuttal seemed so hopeless, and the thicket of misunderstanding between us so old and dense and dusty, that it was less exhausting simply to be as reckless, cynical, and frivolous as they said I was.

'The way you talk,' said Grace one day, 'you would think we were all no better than animals, each grabbing what we want and never thinking of the other fellow.'

'But isn't that exactly what we do do?'

'It might be exactly what you do.'

'Now, girls,' said my mother.

'And it might be what we all do naturally,' continued Grace, 'but we ought to rise above our natures.'

'And how does one do that, Grace?'

'Girls, girls.'

'You pray for a state of grace.'

'What, grace, Grace?'

'Nora, stop that. You might at least have some respect for the beliefs of others. Mother's and mine.'

'Yes, Nora. It's too bad to have you blaspheming in the house.'

'Oh, come on, Grace. What about this state of grace?'

'It is quite possible,' said poor Grace, with a desperate blush, 'for a state of grace to exist wherein the lion lays down with the lamb.'

Ah, yes, I thought, each turned away from the other in the dark, each gritting his teeth. I did not say it aloud because it hinted at humiliations I was too proud to reveal. All I said was, 'In my opinion, lions should lie down with lions and lambs with lambs. It's asking too much of both otherwise, especially the lion.'

'Girls, if you knew how my head ached.'

Everything was oppressively the same except at night. Grace's husband came home then, and played dominoes with my mother, while Grace cooked, and I read aloud to my nephew Peter. Peter, then seven years old, became my favourite member of the family in two seconds by jumping into the big firewood box under the house and shouting, 'Lost in the wood!' After he came home from school I would go with him to the creek to catch yabbies, and as I sat there with my slacks rolled up and my bare feet in the mud, while the sun beat down and the she-oaks soughed, and I exchanged with Peter an occasional low remark, and the yabbie in the silent water drifted upwards to the suspended bait, I would experience the deep poignancy of a recapitulation of childhood sensations that one believes will be one's last.

Peter's memories of those occasions are very different. 'Are you still striking blows for mercy?' the grown man asked me when he came to London after the war.

'I have never struck a blow for mercy in my life.'

'Yes, you have. Don't you remember saying, "Let's strike a blow for mercy", and throwing all those yabbies back?'

I went to see Mrs Partridge, who showed me her collection of masks from New Guinea and gave me Olive's address in London. I wanted to visit Dorothy Rainbow, but was deterred by Grace's protest that it would be stupid, and that I hardly knew her, and that she had no time these days for chatter. But one day, from a tram, I saw her coming out of a shop, carrying a basket. Age had changed but not destroyed her beauty. Her extreme thinness made apparent the elegance of her structure, and blue shadows had appeared on her temples. But her hair had been cut and compressed into a corrugated cap, and in place of the long flowing dresses in which she had moved with such grace, she wore a tight wool skirt and a tight knitted jumper. The result was an uneasy blend of the exotic and the commonplace, and her body, as if confused by these conflicting edicts, moved nervously and abruptly.

'Dorothy looks much better without that great mass of hair,' said my mother comfortably.

I no longer felt those surges of strength, nor the intimation of that presence at my side. I had promised to stay for two weeks, and to cut my visit short would have offended my mother and Grace even more than my presence did. So, with the help of my nephew, I endured it, and, with the help of their righteousness, so did they, but I am sure they were as relieved as I when the time came for me to go.

On the soles of my shoes I slithered across the verandah, ran down the steps. And there was the yellow taxi in the street . . .

Having gone to so much trouble to deceive them about my feelings, I should not have been made so bitter by my success. On the long train journey back to Sydney, torpid and exhausted, I kept hearing those three words—reckless, cynical, frivolous.

Reckless I was, and cynical and frivolous I sometimes felt, but even at the very top of that bent, even as I was walking up the gangplank of the ship, with a tiny hat clamped to one side of my silly head, I was weighted by a sub-stratum of sadness. I knew that like fruit affected by hard drought, I was likely to be rotten before ripe. Sometimes I believed it was already too late, but at others I was seized by a desperate optimism that expressed itself in spates of chatter and laughter and hectic activity.

Ida Mayo and the watercolourist came to the ship, and Colin sent a bunch of roses with a card on which he had written 'No hard feelings.' 'They're like bloody pink cabbages,' I said, and threw them overboard. Ida and the watercolourist looked shocked.

Those roses, as I see them now, rocking on the thick green water of the dockside, do pose a question. Although I still believe that Colin sent them to demonstrate his nobility to Pearl, and although at the time I could feel, almost as if I were there, the exudation of his self-satisfaction as he wrote 'no hard feelings', other reasons do occur. I consider regret, even shock at the realization of how we had wasted each other. And because I can still ask the question, I must ask another. Have I given an accurate account of Colin Porteous, or have I merely provided another substitute? At number six our speculation on the roses always ended in laughter.

'Well, it was certainly very *cryptic* of Colin.'

Perhaps the real man has been so overscored by laughter that he will never be retrieved. As a rule, when we can't find even one good quality in a person, we are prejudiced, and by that rule I must admit my prejudice. Pearl may have been able to mine seams in him disregarded by me, or may have been practical enough to disregard the ones I mined. She certainly would have had a better chance of happiness with him than I had. According to Una Porteous, she had money of her own.

And she was pretty, too, in her outsize way—not fat, but with a large frontal area and a strikingly large face. Liza had a dinner service, with outsize plates, that she used to call her Pearl china. 'Now at last Col will be able to have children,' said Una Porteous. But I am fairly certain he didn't, because, when I left the ship at Southampton, I was pregnant.

He was a middle-aged, squat-bodied American, of considerable honesty and charm. He began by making me laugh, and laughter weakened me easily to love. Hilda, out of her varied experience, used to say that of all aphrodisiacs, laughter is the one most unjustly ignored, and I, out of my limited experience, my very limited experience, used always to agree.

He was an engineer who had been engaged in bridge building in Australia, and awaiting him in England were his wife and two eldest children. With five children already, he was delighted by my barrenness. I didn't have a cabin to myself, and he did, so it was in his cabin that we made love. But it was usually on deck that we talked, walking slowly in our engrossment, and sometimes, in disagreement or perplexity, drifting of one accord to the ship's rail to rest on our folded forearms and resume our detailed, halting exploration of one another. Neither of us had ever known anyone resembling the other, and this exploration so thoroughly engrossed us that when we sat in one of the great public rooms of the ship, it occasionally happened that we realized only by the silence spreading around us that we had forgotten to go down to lunch. By this time I had read a great deal about love affairs, but again my knowledge had been theoretical, and it came as a surprise to me that the reality far surpassed the theory.

'None of those books ever said,' I told him, 'that it was such a marvellous way of getting to know people.'

He looked at me sideways. 'Think of the people you will get to know, now that you are free.'

'Oh, I shall.'

He grimaced slightly, but said, 'Yes, you will.'

In those days the voyage lasted for six weeks. One day in the Mediterranean he remarked that if he had been free he would have liked to marry me. It is an easy thing for a man to say in such circumstances, but because he was not a man who said easy things, but rather who scrupulously avoided them, I believed him, and in retrospect, I still do. All the same, I would have been afraid to marry him. I felt it was precisely the absence of a future together that enabled us to love without cruel possessiveness. The voyage was peaceful, with calm seas and skies, and as day succeeded day, and I continued to keep this friend and lover by my side, and to wake up each morning to the instant realization of his presence in the ship, I grew incredulous of so much luck and happiness, and would not have dared to risk it by extending it further. The definite break on arrival—goodbye and no addresses—was at my insistence, and the argument it caused confirmed me in it.

'You see?' I said. 'Now we are almost quarrelling. The only way to keep these things intact is to give them up.'

'You are either a mad pessimist,' he said, 'or a mad perfectionist. I don't know which.'

'I am neither. I am a preservationist.'

He threw back his head and laughed and laughed. I grew angry and walked away. He caught up with me and walked at my side.

'But what you are preserving?'

'This.'

'But if you have your way it will be over. You will be preserving nothing.'

When I continued to insist, and he to oppose me, we had a real quarrel, followed by a reconciliation during which I wept, and he agreed at last to my terms of goodbye and no addresses.

His wife came down to Southampton to meet him. He had not expected her, and his disconcertion on seeing her on the wharf below, his quick glance from her to me, made me say, 'You see, *this* is what it would be like.' They were the last words I ever said to him. I moved away and stood at another part of the rail.

I saw them later as we passed through the customs. I passed them without turning my head, but I heard her pleasant southern voice, and his reply, and saw out of the tail of my eye that he had also resisted turning to look at me. Against all logic, I suddenly felt discarded. It was a bleak moment, but my cowardly spirit was consoled by not having put him to any sort of test. And I was consoled as well by gratitude for what he had taught me. I believed that our candour and loving freedom had shown me a happy sexual pattern by which I could live. At last, I thought, I knew how freedom could be reconciled with appeasement.

Six weeks later, certain of pregnancy, I remembered Daff and the abortion car. 'As easy as puff,' I remembered her saying. 'The police are fixed. All you need is about fifty pounds and the doctor's address.'

I had money, but no address. However, I thought that if it was as easy as puff in provincial Sydney, it would be even easier in metropolitan London. I was amazed, when I asked Olive Partridge about it, to learn that abortion in London was a matter of whispers, danger, and solemn secrecy.

'They enforce the law here,' said Olive. 'If I got you an address we could both go to jail. Why not have it and let it be adopted?'

But immediately we both cried, 'No!' And then Olive said, 'No, of course not. I'm sorry, Nora. Oh, Lord, this is dreadful. You know, I do think you should get in touch with, er, the man.'

But when I told her of my resolution to make a complete

break, and why I had made it, she began to nod her head even before I had finished speaking. I think her approval was rather literary. She probably thought it gave the event a nice shape. But still, she gave it.

'Let me think,' she said. We were sitting one at each end of the sofa in her living room. She frowned as she thought and chewed one side of her underlip.

The green wraith evoked by her novels had evaporated as soon as I saw her again. Her face was attractive in its mobility and intelligence, but she wore stodgy clothes and had put on weight round the hips and bottom. When I told her about the green wraith she had been both amused and annoyed. 'One day,' she had said, 'I'll write a novel about a woman who looks her best sitting behind a desk. Then no one will be surprised when they meet me.' While she sat and frowned and chewed her underlip, I got up and went to the window and looked down at the trees in Cadogan Square. I was repelled by the stony look of London, its chilly regularity. 'But oh,' I kept saying, 'the trees!' But though the trees, the soft green cumulus of the English trees, moved me to rapture, it was the rapture of an audience who would soon leave the theatre. In Cadogan Square the trees were enclosed by an iron railing with a locked gate. Behind me Olive said slowly, 'There is one woman I know.'

I went back and sat on the sofa again. 'I *think* she may be able to get an address,' said Olive.

'I shan't persuade you to ask her,' I said. 'I should hate you to go to gaol.'

'You sound sarcastic,' said Olive.

'I don't mean to.'

'Off-hand, then. I don't quite know how to take you these days, Nora. I hardly ever know whether you're joking or not. You say everything in such an off-hand way.'

'I'll try not to,' I said.

Olive chewed her lip again, and I waited again. Then she

said with sudden resolution, 'I'll ask this woman, of course. It's only that it's so frightfully embarrassing. She'll think it's for me.'

I was amazed that she should care. Here was another problem of reconciliation. Her novels were so worldly, her 'approved' characters so far above the current moral laws.

'Olive,' I said, 'what do your characters use?'

'Use?'

'What contraceptives? They have affairs, so they must use something, unless the men are sterile or the women barren. And they're not, because they have children, or talk of having them. And what about Aldous Huxley's characters? And Noel Coward's? And D. H. Lawrence's? Yes, his. What do they use?'

'You had better ask them,' said Olive.

'I can't. But I can ask you. What do yours use?'

'I haven't the faintest idea. Contraception—the avoidance of pregnancy—simply is not part of my theme.'

'What is your theme?'

'I suppose,' said Olive, sounding shyer still, 'the delicate nuances of feeling, you know, between a man and a woman in that position. I mean,' she amended quickly, 'in that relationship.'

'But wouldn't those delicate nuances be affected by what they use? You can't tell me it isn't a nuance all of its own if a man has to stop to put something *on*, or a woman has to stop to put something *in*.'

But now Olive gave a laughing shriek and put both hands over her ears. And as I watched her laughing, and shaking her imprisoned head from side to side, I began to laugh myself. I could hardly believe that I should be shocking her (of all people!) in exactly the same way that the first lot of artists used to shock me at Bomera.

'I know what your characters do,' I said in the consciously 'tough' tone of the artists. 'They get pregnant, and have abortions, and I bet you get addresses for them.'

She got the address in a few days. She rang me at my lodgings in Torrington Square, but 'thought it better not to say anything on the phone'.

We met next day in Oxford Street. 'I'm sure she thought it was for me,' said Olive.

We went to an A.B.C. cafe. 'Jean—that's what we'll call the friend who gave it to me—Jean said he charged her a hundred and fifty pounds.'

I clapped a hand to my cheek. 'A hundred and fif—'

'Ssshhh!' We waited until a waitress had passed, then she leaned across the table and whispered, 'And she said to make up a good story, so he'll have an excuse for doing it.'

'An excuse *as well!*'

The doctor was a short thin sallow man with little faded eyes set in huge blue sockets. He wore a black jacket and striped pants, and after confirming my pregnancy he sat with his hands folded and questioned me severely about my motives. How I longed for Doctor So-and-so and his abortion car. Trying not to sound off-hand, I told him there was madness in my family, and after pursing his mouth, and hooding his eyes, and pretending to consider, he rose and said, 'Very well, come tomorrow morning at ten, and bring three hundred pounds.'

I said to Olive, '*Three hun—*'

'Ssshhh!' We were in a cafe again. 'It's those clothes,' said Olive.

'Three hundred,' I whispered. 'I'll have to find someone else.'

But I was almost twelve weeks pregnant, and 'Jean', when telephoned, told Olive that there was no time to find anyone else. Olive offered to come with me, but she was in such a state of nerves that for her sake I refused. She bravely insisted, however, and the next day we went together to the doctor's rooms.

We had been waiting for five minutes when I saw that she

had turned a sickly white and that sweat had collected on her upper lip. She turned miserable eyes to mine.

'I wish I were anywhere but here.'

I thought she would faint. 'Then you should not be here,' I said curtly. 'You had better go.'

'I would never forgive myself.' She took out a handkerchief and dabbed her lips. 'How do you feel?'

'Wonderful.'

'How could you?'

'It's the madness in my family.'

She started to laugh, but I tapped her shoulder and pointed to the inner-communicating door. Behind the glass panel the shadow of a head and shoulders had appeared.

I think if there was madness in anyone's family, it was in his. He spoke with an almost wild contempt. 'Take off your pants. Get up there. Do this. Do that.' There was no anaesthetic of any kind. He strapped my ankles to his contraption and began. 'Stop that noise. Don't tell me it hurts. Of course it hurts. You were willing enough to have the fun, weren't you? Oh, yes! But now you're groaning because it hurts. Hurts! You women. You make me sick, the whole rotten lot of you. There's only one sure way to avoid pregnancy, but oh no, you haven't the decency for that ...'

When he unstrapped me, and I got down, he didn't look at me, but turned to wash his hands and said in the same venomous tone, 'Don't come back here if anything goes wrong. Go to a public hospital. And mention no names.'

In the waiting room Olive whispered, 'Was it terrible?'

She was wide-eyed, and appeared impressed. 'No,' I said angrily, 'it was perfectly all right.'

'When I saw him I thought ...'

'He was quite all right. He was very nice, very kind.'

'You've got mascara all over your cheeks.'

I turned my back to her and removed the mascara with spittle on a handkerchief. We went in silence down the narrow stairs into Charing Cross Road, from where we took a taxi to Olive's flat. I didn't feel in the least faint or ill, but having been told to rest for a few days, I lay on the sofa.

'I bet I know what he used,' I said in my 'tough' voice. 'One of those wire pot cleaners.'

Olive gave a cry and clapped both hands to her ears.

I stayed in her flat, bleeding, for four days. Given her real fear, it was good of her to have me there. When she went out, which she often did, I grew melancholy, but in her presence I was talkative and blithe.

'With what money I have left,' I said one day, 'I think I'll go to a dressmaking school, the best in London, for as long as it takes to become a real professional. Then I'll get a job, and save up until I have enough money to go back to Sydney and work there.'

She nodded approvingly. 'Yes. Go back.'

'What about you?'

She shook her head.

'Why not?'

'I like to live in a country of importance.'

In the mornings, in a rusty-black dressing gown, she would put on her spectacles and worry over various newspapers and periodicals. This was in the second year—or was it the first?—of the Spanish Civil War. 'While you're reading that bit,' I would say, 'give me the clothes bit.'

One morning she said, 'How can you care so much about clothes, Nora, when all *this* is happening?'

'Professional interest.'

'More like sheer gloating.'

'Can't I care about that *and* clothes.'

'Not about this and *so much* about clothes.'

'I didn't know you were a political woman.'

'This isn't political. It is simply,' she said impressively, 'human caring. But in fact,' she added in a lesser tone, 'I happen to be a communist.'

'Really? Lots of people seem to be, nowadays. One is always reading about it. It seems to be quite the thing. But I couldn't, I simply couldn't. Whenever I think of communism I see something grey.'

'That's what you once said about the books I used to read.'

'Grey and flat. Wool, probably, with no weave showing, and a bit bunchy where the sleeves are set in.'

She laughed, but was cross. 'You do it on purpose.'

Again she surprised me; of course I did it on purpose. 'Oh, come on, Ol,' I said. She hated being called Ol. 'Give me the clothes bit.'

She gave it to me with fastidious fingers. 'You're hopelessly frivolous.'

'You sound like Grace.'

'Grace?' She raised her face from her newspaper. 'Your sister,' she said reflectively. 'How *is* Grace?'

'Trying to be religious.'

'That's interesting. What form does it take?'

'Just a sort of churchy Anglican. What's interesting about that?'

'I have a theory that the Protestant tradition in Australia is so tepid that most Australian Protestants lapse into a sort of pantheism. Don't you agree?'

'I might,' I said, 'if I knew what pantheism was.'

In my tone was an echo (I heard it with dismay) of the old growled-out question 'Who does she think *she* is?'

The third day, Saturday, Olive went to one of her meetings. I was dozing when I heard the sound of tennis in the square.

At first I thought the thud of balls must be the remnant of a dream, but when I opened my eyes it still persisted. I went to the window and saw through the trees those moving fragments of white. I shut the window, went back to the sofa, and put a cushion over my head. But I could hear it still.

On the next day, after telling Olive that the bleeding had quite stopped, I returned to my lodgings in Torrington Square. The bleeding had increased, in fact, to the point where I feared involvement for Olive. In a few days there was a flooded bed, a partial confession to a furious and disgusted landlady, and a spoilt mattress to be paid for. Years later I learned from women's gossip that there must have been a fragment of placenta left behind, but at the time I had no idea what was causing it. My mother had thought it indecent to speak of such matters, and in our physiology lessons at school our teacher had given the impression that the body from waist to groin was occupied only by a neatly drawn pelvic girdle, though organs abounded else-where. As for my adult knowledge of the reproductive organs, being gained mostly from sensation, it was woefully simplistic and imprecise.

Though very frightened in that room in Torrington Square, I was prepared to die rather than submit myself to medical examination. I mean that quite literally: I was prepared to die. But the bleeding stopped at last, and never again did I have any sexual contact, of any kind, with anyone.

This long restraint was variously interpreted by the people who knew of it or guessed it, the two most common expla-nations being that I was frigid or an unconscious Lesbian. I was not frigid, and I worked with too many Lesbians for any such tendency on my part to have remained unconscious. No, it was simply, at first, that I was frightened, and for that rea-son avoided the temptation of masculine contact. This gave me habits of stiffness and reticence which in turn deflected the overtures which by that time I may have met. At first it mattered, and then it stopped mattering. 'Compare us,' Hilda used to say. 'All my experience, and all your lack of it. Yet here we are, both old, and what difference has it made, after all?'

By the time I recovered from the abortion I did not have much money left. The first dressmaking academy in which I enrolled proved to be the wrong one, useful only as a source of the gossip that led me to the right one. At the second academy I paid my fees for a year, and then moved to a small room in Maida Vale. Olive pulled a face when she saw it.

'Not very salubrious.'

'Do communists care?'

'This one does.'

'But it's clean. I cleaned it myself. So by salubrious you must mean respectable.'

'I suppose I do. I got a bit of a shock when I saw those women on the ground floor. Not that I don't pity women like that.'

'Olive, you bewilder me.'

'Why, Nora?'

'You might never have left home.'

'It's interesting that you say that. I feel that in myself.' She set one hand on her chest. 'Some block, some point beyond which I can't develop. Do try to explain what you mean.'

But I could not then express my feeling that she had brought with her the contradictions of our home society—its rawness and weak gentility, its innocence and deep deceptions—and had merely given them a slightly different form.

'I think,' she said, looking earnestly at some point beyond my head, 'that I need to lose myself, sink myself.'

'You also need to stop wearing tan shoes with a puce dress.'

'I want to be simple, utterly simple. Like water.'

'No chance. You'll never be simple, and neither shall I. We both had to start disguising ourselves too early.'

She looked at me, half-frowning, half-laughing. 'You know, Nora, you're very intelligent.'

'I know. Isn't it a pity I'm so stupid?'

Of course, I underestimated Olive. If she did not arrive at simplicity in her person, she did so in her later books, whereas I never have, in anything. The different courses on which our lives were already set began to be apparent in those first weeks in London. Her seriousness was a challenge that goaded me to flippancy, and from my flippancy, she, in her turn, defended herself by a seriousness which became at each of our meetings more flat and assertive. She herself disliked it.

'I didn't mean to put it like that. I'm talking like an earnest school girl. But I just can't think how else to put it.'

And nor could I think how else to put it but by my brazen levity. I remarked one day that if our characters could have been combined we may have made between us one good person. But Olive stared at me, and slowly shook her head.

'Not in my sense of the word good.'

But we remained friends in spite of these clashes, and when she had a success with her third novel, and went to live in France, I felt very much alone. And yet, in many ways, I was glad to be alone. I had entered once more on a period of waiting. A number of the artists from Bomera, from both the first and the last lot, had drifted to London, and occasionally I would encounter one of them, and we would talk of the harbour, the sun, and the cicadas in the plane trees in Macleay Street.

'I'm going back for certain,' I would say. 'But I have to wait until I've finished this course and can save some money.'

Whenever I met them, the talk was always of who was going and who was staying. The declaration of one man I often repeated later, and the words he used passed into my vocabulary.

'If you stay more than five years you become a pommiefied Aussie, than which there is no more pitiful creature on God's earth. Unless it's an aussiefied Pom, and that's how you feel when you try to go back.'

But for some the issues were simpler and more physical. England was a nasty dank little country, they said, where the people were unfriendly, the sky was low, and life was a misery for all but the rich.

Certainly, for me at that time, the air of London seemed mysteriously inimical to friendship. I made casual acquaintances of a couple who lived in the same house, but when I moved to a room on the other side of the canal, a cold attic in Westbourne Terrace Road, I saw them no more. I worked very hard at classes, and again made a few acquaintances in the house. I kept moving from house to house in the same area, first to Warwick Crescent, which I liked because it was on the canal, and then to Warwick Avenue, which I liked because it wasn't, and then to various other places, but always in that same little part of London. Every time I moved, I made new acquaintances in the house, and stopped seeing the last lot. And either at classes or in the houses, I would find a lesser Lewie.

With him, I would walk in parks, go to pubs, and shop on Saturdays. Of our Saturday shopping we always made a little treat. The Portobello Road was just another market then, and we would buy baskets of cress, tomatoes from the Canary Islands, Australian butter and cheese cheaper than at home, second-hand books, and sometimes, at the stalls past the eel tanks, an old dress buckle, some beads or a belt. On Sundays we usually caught Greenline coaches into the country, but if it were raining, or the east wind blew, I used to stay in bed the whole of Sunday and read the books I had bought in the Portobello Road.

I had conceived a gloomy passion for ancient history, and since one thing leads to another, I soon knew what pantheism was. I wrote to Olive and told her so. In her reply she told me she was no longer a communist ('*You were right about that grey coat*') and that she had met an Austrian doctor of philosophy and was going to live with him in Vienna. I wrote and asked if that would make her simple, and she replied that she thought it very likely.

'*He is very serious. You would laugh at him, or perhaps not. In any case, he has amplified my life as no one else has done. I see now how mechanical my life was, and my writing as well.*'

Our correspondence started to peter out about a year later, when she wrote that she had great difficulty in replying to my letters. I am not sure to this day whether that note of helplessness was invoked by her expanding powers, my persistent levity, or by some change in her character or circumstances unimaginable by me. When I remember her shaking her head and saying, 'Not in my sense of the word good,' I feel I am close to an answer, but still it evades me, and it is still with a tantalizing sense of mystery that I read the affectionate inscriptions in the novels she has never failed to send me. Those inscriptions, and my few lines of thanks, have been our only correspondence for more than thirty years.

In bed on those cold Sundays I also read what David Snow, the most lasting of my Lewies, called 'the great big beautiful classics.' I also found them beautiful. My money ran out long before my course was finished, but by that time I was taking private orders, and although through too much reading and sewing my health suffered and my eyesight deteriorated, I was proud to be keeping myself above the hunger line. I had the curious feeling that this period of hard work and privation had been lying in wait for me for a long time, and to meet it at last, and survive it by my own efforts, gave me intense satisfaction.

Included in this general satisfaction was a particular triumph. Cutting, for which I had so little natural aptitude, had become my greatest skill. I knew I could never acquire the flexible wrist, the ease and certainty that dazzled me in one of my teachers. I had started too late for that. But my awareness of this handicap made me compensate for it in other ways, so that at the end of my course I was able to get a job in a good small place in Grafton Street.

I wrote to Ida Mayo that it was now simply a matter of saving enough money to set me up on my return. *'In about three years,'* I said.

'Perhaps it will be you who employs me,' she wrote back. *'Now wouldn't that be a turn-up for the books?'*

From Grafton Street I moved to one of the big dressmakers. He paid me badly, but I liked working on such celebrated clothes, and I loved the mounting excitement before a showing. Here, at last, I lost interest in my own clothes, and accepted the suit for my uniform. I was thirty-eight. To people who commented on my youthful appearance, I would reply that I was the type that collapses overnight, but I never believed it, not for a moment.

I had lost my distaste for London. The Georgian terraces that had formerly seemed repellently chilly I now saw as formal and peaceful. I never lived in one of them. It was always my luck to find accommodation in houses of a later date, usually Victorian. But these too were spacious and solid. I never once lived in an ill-proportioned room.

When at last I moved out of the little area near the canal where I had shuttled about so much, it was again to a Victorian house. I crossed the Harrow Road to Holland Park, where I found a big room with a kitchen and bath. My liking for London had not affected my deeper attachment to Sydney, and because I meant to return as soon as was practicable, I took the place furnished. But I couldn't resist buying my own curtains, of soft blue velveteen, and a beautifully faded Persian rug. When

the room next to mine became vacant I made a sudden decision. I rented it and went into business for myself.

All my acquaintances, David Snow in particular, advised me
to put up my plate. Brass was the only kind possible. It was ex-
pensive, but would serve for my Sydney business as well. I shall
never forget my first sight of it after it was put up.

NORA PORTEOUS—DRESSMAKER

'I have come a long roundabout way,' I remarked to David,
'to find out who I am.'

He was always quick to catch my moods. He put a consoling
arm across my shoulders. 'We should open champagne.'

From the start I had plenty of customers, and even though I
worked so slowly (another penalty for my late beginning), and
was diffident about charging enough, I was still able to save
money as well as spending several short holidays in Normandy
or Paris. Here Colin Porteous's French grammar books showed
their profit and loss: I could read the French newspapers, but
could not make myself understood by the French people.

On each return to London I would appreciate afresh the
solidity and weight of its buildings, interspersed by the massy
billows or the complex tracery of its trees. But between me
and London, as between me and the people I called my friends
(even David Snow) lay the distance created by my intentions: I
was going home.

When I spoke of David as 'one of my Lewies', I meant in his
relationship with me. He was not like Lewie in character. His
habit of thought was steadier, he was less flippant, and, I think,
less intense.

'Why do you want to go back?' he asked me once.

'Sydney, that part of it, is the only place where I've ever felt
at home.'

'Won't it have changed?'

'Very little, Ida Mayo says.'

'But what about you? You will have changed.'

'I suppose so,' I said vaguely. I didn't want to talk about it, did not want to admit to impediments.

'Some people are homeless wherever they live,' he said. 'You are. And so am I.'

'But you are an Englishman in your own country.'

'I am homeless on this earth,' he said with a smile. 'And so are you. Once you admit it, you know, you'll find it has advantages. The thing is to admit it, and relax, and not be forever straining forward.'

'I am not straining forward. I am waiting, and occupying myself while I wait. Which is quite a different matter. And besides,' I said, to turn the conversation, 'I don't want to live in a climate where they can't grow oranges.'

But although in my determination to go home I showed no outward faltering, my memories of Sydney were becoming less precise. Daydreaming of home while I worked, I would feel myself in a long quiet room, depersonalized by a completeness of physical comfort, my body fused into the atmosphere, into the warmth of the sun and the drone of an eternal noon. Going home, though I did not realize it at the time, had become a project urged less by my mind than my body, which needed sun.

'I bet you never go back,' said David.

'I will. I must. Or I'll become a pommiefied Aussie.'

I booked my passage at last, in March 1939, on a ship that was to sail in November. It did sail, in spite of the declaration of war, but I was in hospital at the time, with the first of my severe bouts of bronchitis.

'I knew you wouldn't go,' said David. 'You got sick on purpose.'

The winter of 1939–40 was extremely severe. Every time I

got on my feet, down I would go again, to lie in bed coughing. Pleurisy set in, and by the time I got out of hospital, weakened and considerably poorer, there were no more passenger ships out.

And so another period of waiting began, but this time I did not wait alone, for who did not live out those war years in the larger context of 'when it is over'? My mother died during the war, and so did Ida Mayo, and so did Grace's husband. David Snow was killed at Dunkirk, and several of my work companions were killed in the raids on London. For four years I made military uniforms, and for six winters I was ill with bronchitis. Some people are strengthened by the trials of war. Olive, who elected to stay with her man in Vienna, was one of them, as is evident from her later books. Perhaps if something else had been required of me than to make military uniforms, I would have been one of them, too. However, it was a time when one did what was required of one, and that was what they required of me.

It was the gentle watercolourist who wrote and told me of Ida Mayo's death. I know his name now. I saw him in a photograph, wearing what looked like the same long dustcoat, in a magazine Betty Cust brought me the other day. It seems that posthumously his work has achieved a small fame. He survived, alone in a cottage in the Blue Mountains, until 1960. His last paintings, said the writer of this article, were lyrical and happy, like the work of a marvellous child.

'Has Lyn Wilmot been this afternoon?' asks Betty Cust.

'Yes,' I say, 'thank you.'

'You're being very patient about it.'

'About Mrs Wilmot?'

'About not being allowed up.'

I make a vague murmur to cover my guilt, because of course it is easy to be patient about Doctor Rainbow's embargo on getting up when one has already disobeyed it, and intends to keep on doing so.

'Well, anyway,' says Betty, 'there's some good news as well. The mail strike's settled.'

'Oh. Wonderful. When may I expect letters?'

'In a day or two, I should think.'

'Then I must start to write some.'

I look through the window and begin to compose a letter to Hilda and Liza.

My dears, there are telegraph poles on one side of this street, and from these poles long black wires extend to the houses, two or three to each pole, for all the world like a small pack of dogs tethered to a post. When I first arrived the visual impression made by all these black wires was horrible, but now ...

'Here is Jack,' says Betty. 'He has been hosing at the back. The water board only lets us hose twice a day, because of the drought.'

Jack comes in, carrying a bunch of chives.

'Anything dead?' asks Betty.

'Nothing. Everything's as good as gold. Which is more than we can say.'

'We think one of our poinciana trees is dying,' says Betty to me.

'Never mind,' says Jack. 'If they all die, the whole darned lot of them, the jacarandas too, then we can go on that trip to Europe. She can't go,' he explains to me, 'because if she goes from October to November, inclusive, she misses the jacaranda in bloom, and if she goes from December to January, inclusive, she misses the poinciana.'

'But,' I say, 'that still leaves most of the year.'

'Well,' says Jack, 'you might be able to persuade her. I can't.'

'Something or other always happens,' murmurs Betty, with a vagueness similar to mine of a few minutes ago. 'One of the children has a baby, or is just about to have one . . .'

'Or one of the babies is just about to walk or talk,' says Jack. 'Or someone has hurt their little toe.'

'I'll go one day,' says Betty.

'Like heck you will,' says Jack.

'Do *you* want to go?' I ask Jack.

He becomes serious at once. 'I wouldn't mind going,' he says cautiously.

Betty gives me a smile, as if to say, 'You see?' She looks up at Jack sideways. 'Jack is going to get your dinner tonight, Nora.'

'Yes,' says Jack, 'because she's going to see someone who's hurt their toe.'

Betty, who is standing with her arms folded, buffets Jack sideways with one hip. 'He's a wonderful cook, Nora.'

'I'm only a snacks cook,' says Jack.

As soon as Betty goes there is a clash of intentions reminiscent of the day of my arrival. He wants to cook a fillet steak, and I want an omelette flavoured with the chives he is holding. I win, and get the omelette, which turns out to be perfect. The chives, he tells me, grow at the foot of the back steps. He gave a few plants to Grace twenty years ago.

'They've just got to the picking stage again. They die back for a couple of months each year.'

'Only a couple of months!'

I am thinking of my little pot of chives at number six. When pondering reasons for returning, I never once thought of the food, the sensuous tropical fruits, and the plentiful vegetable products of the warm earth. I am partly thinking aloud when I say, 'There are compensations in coming back, after all.'

He looks amazed that I should even have doubted it.

I mop up the buttery remains of the omelette with a crust of bread. He watches me with pleasure.

'You are a good cook,' I say, as I hand him the plate.

'I wish you had had the steak,' he says wistfully.

'And you like cooking, I can tell.'

'Oh,' he says, 'I like doing all kinds of things.'

'Gardening? Everyone here seems to like gardening.'

'Yes. But Bet's the real gardener. I hope to God,' he says with sudden intensity, 'that poinciana doesn't die. She'll be upset. I will, too. It was one of the first things Mum planted.'

I think of Mrs Cust, washing her hands with sugar and soap at the kitchen sink, and speaking of what the garden is doing to her hands, while I, with my head sunk to my forearms ...

'Why did I cry,' I ask Jack Cust, 'in the kitchen at the back of your shop?'

'I don't know why, exactly. But I remember you did. Because I was there.'

'Not in the kitchen?'

'Yes. Until Mum shoo'ed me away.'

'Then if it wasn't you playing scales in the sitting room above the shop, who was it?'

'That would have been Arch.'

'Arch?' Again I feel that uneasiness, that sense of danger. 'Was Arch your brother?'

'Yes.' Jack picks up my tray. 'I don't remember exactly, but I think it must have been Arch made you cry. Because I remember afterwards, Dad hauling him over the coals, telling him he wasn't to tease Miss Roche any more. Oh yes,' says Jack, making for the door, 'Arch was a real handful in those days.'

'Wait!' I say. My globe of memory has given one of its lightning spins, and I am dumbfounded not only by what it shows, but by the fact that it has remained on the dark side for so long. Jack has turned back from the door and is looking at me with enquiry.

'You must have been very young then,' I say cautiously.

'I would have been nine.'

'And how old'—I am fearful, but inclined to laugh as well—'how old was Arch?'

'If I was nine, Arch was thirteen.'

Thirteen!

'I don't remember much about Arch,' I say rather curtly.

'I daresay he will come back.'

'Not with my memory.' But of course, he already has. 'Are you sure you were only nine?'

'Sure. Because it was the year we moved from over the shop.'

He leaves with my tray, and from the kitchen I presently hear the sounds of washing up. Thirteen! I was twenty when I used to hear those scales from the sitting room above the shop. The recollection, as if it has gathered strength during its long quiescence in the dark, flows out with amazing clarity and speed, so that my mind must race to grasp it, to hold it down. It was always in the drowsy middle part of the hot days that I used to hear that piano. I see myself prowling about the shop, restless, waiting in suspense for the piano notes to stop and the silence begin to create its own, more painful suspense. The shop was big and darkish and in the hot glare of the wide doorway a customer would occasionally appear and bring me the relief of speech, but I was usually alone, for in the quiet hours from twelve to two the Custs would leave me in charge while they went to work on their new house, the 'big white corner house' to which they were about to move. They took the quiet little boy with the long chin, whom I can identify now as Jack, and left Arch at home to practise in the sitting room above the shop.

To ease my wait I tidied the stock. I made the piles of comics and exercise books as neat as blocks. I picked out broken slate pencils and pieces of chalk and put them in an old shoe box, and inserting my hands into the glass display cases I swung aside the lids of pencil cases to reveal their long interior compartments. The scales ascended and descended, even and impersonal, mocking my angry waiting, my trembling hands. I re-graded pencils displaced by the morning's customers and scrabbled among pen nibs to find and extract the odd-men-out. The scales are becoming less even. I hear the thump, the heavy touch of the thumb. More and more uneven. Up and down the keyboard, up and down, hands rock like crabs. I purse my lips. The stock must be made utterly neat. The pen holders, the tin pencil holders, the crayons, the coloured pencils, all must go in rows. The stiff dimpled paper must be laid again across the baths of watercolour in the black tin paintboxes examined that morning. The scales stop. The blood floods my pink face and sweat flows into my armpits and the palms of my hands. Between my teeth I mutter that he had better not, better not. I am furious in advance, my eyes suffused with tears. The silence extends. I know him! He is sitting on the piano stool, listening to me listening, and grinning. I put a hand over my mouth, pressing firmly on the lips that would grin in response. But when I hear, picked out with one hand, the first six notes of 'Cherry Ripe', laughter spurts out from behind the hand. I give a stifled crow. Laughter is building up in me, up and up, and when I am intolerably crammed with it, I run, bent double, my shoulders jolting, into the back of the shop. The piano stool crashes to the floor above me as I reach the kitchen door, and then I hear the thud of bare feet on the narrow wooden steps, not running, but setting down each foot with a thump of eloquent deliberation. As I turn against the opposite wall of the kitchen, he appears at the turn of the stairs. Exultantly grinning, he bounds from there on to a kitchen chair, and from the chair to the table, where he stands poised to dive on me.

I stand with one hand extended like a policeman's and the other spread over my face, while fury and laughter contend agonizingly within me. Arch is said to be ugly, but like Dorothy Irey, he seems exotic to me. He is broad and squat, his mouth is huge, and his shining white teeth are big and concave. His forehead is low, his cheekbones high, and his eyes mere slits. But his nose, short and delicate, is from quite another type of face.

He leaps. I give a shout of laughter and anger as his arms grip me, and then begins our shuffling panting speechless struggle. He is strong, cunning, and shameless, shepherd boy or young satyr. But we are not in Arcady, and I have long ago been spoilt for or saved from nymphean uses. And besides, he is too young.

Too young. Though succeeding at last in pinning my arms with his, and immobilizing me, he does not quite know what to do next, but rocks me to and fro as if to say, 'Come on! Move! Struggle!' And as soon as I do, he lets me escape, and bounds on the table again, and jumps down again, and makes a few hilarious feints at me, a few tickling rushes, before flopping into a chair and saying in his high sweet voice, 'Hey, Miss Roche, look at your hair. Say if someone came into the shop?'

I am already putting my hair up. 'All right, Arch,' I say in a shaking voice, 'you've had your last chance.'

'You won't pimp,' he says with confidence.

'The moment your father gets home.'

He laughs.

'I mean it,' I say. 'I have asked you and asked you, but you take no notice.'

'Then why do you come running into the back?'

'How can I stay in the front, laughing like that?'

'What makes you laugh?'

I don't remind him of how it all began, of how he used to stop practising, and creep silently down the stairs, and through the kitchen, and into the shop, and leap on me from behind. It is beneath my dignity to explain the nervous expectation this trick has implanted in me. 'I am not discussing it any more, Arch,' I say. 'This time I am acting.'

'Jeez,' says Arch, 'all I do is stop for a bit of a rest. It's you who starts it. You run in here because you *want* me to come down.'

'Oh!' I am furious. He has gone too far. He has breached an unspoken rule. 'How *dare* you!'

He bursts into laughter, jumps up, and comes at me again with his feinting, slapping, prodding, tickling. But I can no longer allow mirth to modify my anger. If my anger remains strong and real, it will give me back my dignity. I await my chance, get past his guard, and slap him like a mother. I am reinforcing the weak shield of my anger by humiliating him.

'Leave me alone,' I say with adult contempt. 'You! A boy in short pants!'

He continues to dodge about me, laughing and flicking me with blows, but now something cruel and serious is taking place between us. No longer disabled by laughter, quick and watchful, I make my way past him and run into the shop. I hear him race up the stairs. The piano stool grates across the floor, and the first notes are struck. I run to my purse, take out my handkerchief, and hold it to my face. Steadily and silently, I weep for relief and shame, while the notes, regular again, sound in my ears as alternately impudent and pathetic.

'See! You didn't tell,' he would say next day.

'I am giving you one last chance.'

One day he tickled me in the presence of his mother. 'Arch, Arch,' she said absently. She was counting and balancing the money, a job quite rightly considered outside my scope. I hit him. 'It's only his fun, Nora. Twenty-two, twenty-three, twenty-four . . . Stop that at once, Arch. How do you expect me to count?'

These public teasings were his insurance, I knew, in case

I should reveal his private ones. 'It's only his fun, Nora,' his mother could then continue to say. And that is almost exactly what happened. One day in our wrestling he butted his face against my breast and at the same time held me so tightly that I could not make him let go. The top of his head was beneath my chin. His black curls had been cut off long ago, but I was familiar with the whorls that remained, and in a moment of tender dazed silence I set my cheek against his head to trace on my skin the base of those absent curls. He immediately pulled my blouse apart, set his curved teeth in my shoulder, and gave a man's groan, and I then gave a great tearing sob, which rose to a scream, and frightened him, and made him let me go.

Tears were my only legitimate alleviation, and this time I gave way to them completely. With my forearms on the kitchen table, and my forehead pressed on to them, I sobbed and sobbed, while he stood at my side, my little Arcadian lover, pushing a glass of water against my arm and saying respectfully, 'Drink this. Drink this. Drink this.'

When the shop bell rang, and he ran out to serve the customer, I staggered from my chair, shut both doors between myself and the shop, and returned to continue my crying. This action gave him the mistaken idea that my crying was wholly voluntary. 'Well,' he said awkwardly, 'it's two o'clock. You're all right now, so I'll go back up.' Through my quieter sobs I heard the receding thud of his feet on the stairs, but when I heard the ascending scale of piano notes, so impersonal, so remote, I was driven into the deeper paroxysm in which Mr and Mrs Cust discovered me. It was Arch, I sobbed, banging the table with my forehead. Arch, Arch, Arch. 'Oh, now then, Nora,' said Mrs Cust in reproach, 'it's only his fun.'

'Arch does tease, though,' she said to her husband.

'You're right, he does. I'll speak to him.'

To soothe me, they spoke soothingly to each other. While

letting me 'have my cry out', they discussed in lullaby tones
the planting of trees at the new house, and when the notes upstairs began to stumble and thump, Mrs Cust gave a crooning
discourse on Arch's heavy thumb, and Mr Cust replied with
tranquility that it was high time she damn well realized it was
a waste of money, and that he was too old to learn. The scales
stopped at last, Arch ran down the stairs and out of the back
door to join a group of friends, and I stopped crying, got up,
and said dully, 'I'm sorry.'

When I rejoined Olive in the abortionist's waiting room I
told her he had been very nice, very kind. When I rose to face
the Custs I kept a hand over the torn buttonholes of my blouse.
But not to spare Arch. I spare nobody or nothing but my own
pride. The springs of my shame were not in morality. A boy in
short pants! On the following day Arch was enlisted to help
with the moving. The move was over in two days, I left the shop
to work in town, and I never saw him at close quarters again.
In fact, I remember seeing him so seldom, even in the distance,
that I am looking for another explanation than that I slammed
a door on the incident, and sent my shame into hiding, though
I certainly did that as well. I wait with impatience for Jack Cust
to finish washing up in the kitchen, and as soon as he appears
in the doorway, rolling down his sleeves, I ask him what became
of Arch.

'Ah. You've remembered him.'

'Yes.'

'I knew you would. He's done pretty well, Arch has. Lovely
home he has up in Cairns. Lovely.'

'No, I meant what became of him after you stopped living
over the shop. I can't recall seeing him about much after that.'

'You mightn't have. They sent him to boarding school when
he was fourteen, and to Mum's brother out west for most of
the holidays. Thought it might quieten him down a bit, all the

discipline and hard work. But it did no good. He was always in trouble.'

'What kind of trouble?'

'Girls. It was always girls. He got married young, got divorced, went right through the war in the army, and then came home and started chasing after a girl of eighteen. He was thirty-nine. Everyone—Mum and Dad, everyone, told him he was mad. Everyone except the girl. She married him like a shot. And you might say they lived happily ever after. Which just proves what I always say, that with these things you can never tell.'

'I'm glad things turned out so well for him.'

'Everybody is. Arch had a way with him.'

'I seem to remember he had.'

'Everybody liked Arch.'

'Did Grace like him?'

'Yes, even Grace. Though she always used to call his wife "that poor little girl".'

'Was she pretty, that poor little girl?'

'The image of you as a girl, according to Grace.'

'How strange.'

But I don't think it strange at all. I remember the man I loved on the voyage to London, his broad body, wide cheekbones, and the big concave teeth displayed by his frequent laughter.

'Well,' says Jack Cust, 'I'll push off. Lyn Wilmot will be here any tick of the clock.' But before he goes he says, 'It was Arch sent that pawpaw down, the one ripening in the kitchen. He grows them. Not for a living, he gets most of his living from fishing, he's got a first-rate trawler. But he grows more fruit than they need, and every now and again, when he's got a mate driving down, he sends us a case.'

'I shall eat the pawpaw with added pleasure,' I say with a smile.

I continue to smile after he goes, extending the amused

indulgence of old age to that foolish young woman and that boy. I speculate on what would have happened if I had met him again when we were both adults—say, on the visit I made before sailing for London. It could easily have happened. I imagine myself sitting beside the creek with my nephew, listening to the she-oaks and watching the yabbie rising to the bait suspended in the muddy water. I look up suddenly, and see him standing there. But of course, his face is now the face of my ship-board lover.

Later that day, it occurs to me to wonder what they would have made of Arch at number six. And I find I am glad, very glad, that I did not recall him in time to expose him. I believe there were times when I very nearly did so, because I remember that when we talked of jobs we had had, work we had done when young, I never once mentioned having worked in a newsagent's and stationer's shop. And I remember too that this avoidance, and my impulse to change the subject, used always slightly to puzzle me. I knew it was not snobbery—my snobberies were never of that sort—and even as I diverted the flow of the conversation, I mentally charted those little snags of perplexity, so that 'one day' I could return on my tracks to examine and resolve them.

But I never did so, and Arch stayed on the dark side, and now I can be glad that he was never overlaid by the discussion, speculation, and humour that will always bring uncertainty to my view of Colin Porteous.

I feel well when I wake the next morning—better than I have felt since that April day when Fred climbed the steps to tell us about his burgundy. Last night Lyn Wilmot pulled my arm roughly as she helped me out of bed, and was angry when I laughed. I could not explain that my amusement was caused by being made to suffer for help I neither needed nor wanted, so I said nothing, and she—perhaps ashamed—was gentler when she 'helped' me back to bed.

It is time I ended the farcical situation by announcing that if I am not allowed to get up today, I shall do so on my own responsibility, but as I get out of bed and put on my robe and slippers, I confess to a regret, for there is no doubt that surreptitious disobedience gives me a slight but distinct pleasure—a legacy, perhaps, from my marriage.

In the bathroom mirror I look with equanimity at an old woman with a dewlapped face and hands like bunches of knotted sticks. I lean calmly to the cool water. Well, I am what I am. The tenderness and indulgence stirred by the recollection of Arch still lingers in me. I forgive myself everything.

After I have washed I go to the kitchen and inspect the china. Small dead moths lie in their own powder at the bottom of Grace's best cups. They are part of a tea service, not at all bad, that occupies an isolated cupboard alone. I look forward to washing it and bringing it into everyday use. This is not the time to keep anything 'for best'.

I find some over-ripe strawberries and eat them at the kitchen sink so that juice will not run down my chin. And now a quaking comes over me, and an exhaustion and faintness that would make me feel rather desperate, if I let it. On the way back to bed, to prove in the face of it that I am still in my happy exploratory mood, I make a detour and throw open the door of my old bedroom.

I wish I hadn't. There amidst broken chairs, cartons piled high with books, a washstand with a cracked marble top, dilapidated suitcases and dress baskets, stands my old bed—narrow, long-legged, with a fringed quilt flung over the lumpy mattress and hanging nearly to the floor. It is comical enough, resembling a medieval horse in a school play, but the fact that

it is not dismantled disturbs me. Common sense tells me that
Grace must have kept it here in case she wanted to put some
poor soul up in it, perhaps one of the overflow of Tom Chiddy's
country cousins, but I still cannot get rid of my first impression
on opening the door: that it has been standing there all this
time, waiting for me, and that by coming into its presence I
have walked into the trap I sensed (or imagined) two years ago,
when Peter Chiddy, sitting in one of my little yellow chairs at
number six, told me that Grace had left the house to him, but
had stipulated that it must not be sold in my lifetime in case I
should want to occupy it. The proposal had aroused me to a
quick but elusive resentment, an echo of my old resistance to
Grace's domineering ways, and to her censure of my determination to leave home. 'She's still trying!' was my interior cry. I
refused without hesitation, rising out of the second yellow chair
to make my point more definite.

'Sell it, Peter dear, sell it.'

Peter also rose. He put both hands on my arms. 'Don't
make up your mind yet. Think, Aunt Nora. You pay rent here, I
suppose?'

'Of course.'

'There'll be none there. And rates and maintenance are to be
taken care of. Dad left mother well off, you know. So you see,
Aunt Nora, with the pension, and the bit you have . . .'

'Peter, sell it. If you need my permission, you have it.'

'I can't, even then. Not in your lifetime.'

'Then rent it, my dear, rent it.'

'No. You may change your mind. I think you will.'

But I smiled, and shut my eyes, and shook my head slowly
from side to side.

'Never! I assure you! Never!'

I open the top left-hand drawer in my old dressing table,
where I once kept stockings and scarves, and find it stacked

with albums. As I take out the top one a big photograph falls to the floor. I know before I pick it up and turn it over that I shall see my father's face.

Once, standing at Colin Porteous's side, I had examined it with greedy bewildered curiosity. I examine it in the same way now, holding it close to my eyes and re-setting my spectacles on my nose. But the more pleadingly I stare, the more expressionless, the more impersonal, that young fair face becomes.

With the photograph still in my hand, I am shutting behind me the door of that disturbing room, when I hear footsteps on the front stairs. Taken by surprise, I forget my resolve to 'end the farcial situation', and go as fast as my weakness allows me, with an absurd schoolgirl sense of being 'almost caught', into my bedroom and back into bed.

'You *are* early this morning.'

'Yes,' says Doctor Rainbow. He is looking at me searchingly. Was my voice breathless? Have I strawberry juice on my chin? I am still holding the photograph of my father. I put it under the magazines on the lower shelf of my bedside table.

'You look very well,' he says. 'I think we may let you up today.'

To reply that I have already been up would be to make a fool of the man. I have no alternative but to express delight. He examines me. He remarks that my temperature continues to be normal. He picks up my wrist and looks at the healed scratch.

'Very good. I'll call at the Custs' as I pass and ask Betty to come and get you up.'

'Betty is *good*,' I say. 'She makes me wish I had never used the word for anything else, but had kept it just for her.'

'Yes, she's very good. Don't walk around, will you? Stay in a chair.'

'But I may go to the bathroom alone?'

'Well, as long as you go straight there and back.'

'This is a red letter day for me,' I cannot help saying.

As he is going he drops a parcel on my bed. 'Betty asked me to let you see this. No hurry to give it back.'

I open it as soon as he goes. I was once persuaded to make an embroidery for a charity raffle. It was won by Dorothy Rainbow, and there it is—a swag of jacaranda leaves with the head and breast of a big magpie thrusting through. It supports my suspicion that the orange tree was a fluke, for although the conception is good, it is muddled in execution. I suspect it was something I actually saw, and tried, with mistaken fidelity, to reproduce.

'Not nearly so good as the other,' I tell Betty when she comes.

'Well! Why sound so pleased about it? Doesn't she sound pleased about it, Jack?'

Jack picks up the embroidery. 'Looks pretty good to me. What's wrong with it?'

'It proves the other was a fluke.'

'Or that this one is,' says Betty, 'if it's as bad as you say.'

She takes the embroidery from Jack and looks at it attentively. 'You must be terribly fussy, Nora,' she says in a disappointed voice. 'It's always been my favourite. You would think that maggie was real.'

The criteria of even the most trivial art are not those of virtue. How often must one remind oneself of this, and hold one's carping tongue? I take the embroidery and say, 'It's very dusty, isn't it? Nobody has cared for it. Wouldn't you think one of Dorothy's daughters would have taken it? Doctor Rainbow isn't married, is he?'

'No,' says Jack, 'nor likely to be.'

'Breakfast first, Nora,' says Betty. 'Then we'll get you up.'

But Jack continues. 'Not after seeing his mother like that.'

'Oh, *Jack*!' says Betty.

Jack shows alarm. He points at me, but looks at Betty. 'Doesn't she . . . Doesn't Nora . . . ?'

'I did *tell* you, Jack.'

'Betty,' I say, 'I am not so easily distressed as you appear to think. I guessed it was suicide. It was suicide, I take it?'

Betty sighs. 'Yes, it was.'

'He saw her with her head in the gas oven.'

The eager propitiation in Jack's voice makes it seem, oddly, as if by this disclosure he means to make amends for his first indiscretion. Betty gives him one of those looks that are such a comfort to the unmarried. 'Betty,' I say, almost laughing, 'suicide doesn't shock me.'

But by her frown, and her refusal to look at Jack, I see that she is still annoyed with him. 'What would you like for breakfast, Nora?'

After breakfast, while Jack is bringing a long chair from some other part of the house, I draw her fire by telling her I have already been up. And she frowns again, and now won't look at me. But I will distract her from both Jack and myself.

'And I went into my old bedroom, and found this.' I take the photograph of my father from between the magazines. 'Imagine! I was six when my father died. And all I remember of him is this photograph.'

'Really?'

'Yes. Absolutely all. The photograph has swallowed the man.'

'But Grace said your grief when he died was quite excessive.'

'Grace thought everything about me was quite excessive.'

'Perhaps your grief swallowed the man.'

'Then it swallowed itself as well. I remember no grief.'

Jack comes back with the chair. 'Jack,' says Betty, all crossness forgotten, 'look, this is Nora's father.'

After they go, I sit in the chair, with a rug over my knees, and examine the embroidery. My chair is by the window, and as I handle the embroidery particles of dust detach themselves from it and hang in the sunlight. Unsuccessful though it is, I

am offended by this dust. I begin to form an uncompliment-
ary image of Dorothy's daughters—heedless women, carrying
cartons of groceries to their cars, sunburnt, bossy, busy, half-
naked, not caring at all that their mother's things should be
left to the care of a busy bachelor. I know now how Dorothy
killed herself, but should still like to know why, and am sorry
that the suspended conflict between the Custs prevented me
from asking. It is strange that whenever I hear of a suicide I feel
compelled to ask 'Why?' and 'How?' although I know from my
own experience that the cause can be hard to define, and that
the means tend to be those nearest to hand—in Dorothy Rainbow's case, a gas oven, and in mine, sleeping pills, because they
were always there, in the drawer of my bedside table. As for the
reason, I can say that in my body and spirit a spark seemed to
have been extinguished, but I must still ask what put out that
spark, and if I leap to explain that the weakness resulting from
six bronchial winters, and the approach of the menopause, left
me morbidly defenceless against the postwar revelations of the
German camps, it is because I am ashamed to admit that in the
same breath as that vast horror, I can speak of the loss of my
looks. Whether that loss alone would have reduced my world to
greyness I cannot say, but I do distinctly recollect that on those
rare days when my spirit triumphed over my face, and I looked
well again, the horrors of the camps pressed lighter upon me.

'I am the type that collapses overnight,' I used to reply to
those compliments on my youthful appearance. And so it
turned out. Overnight, it seemed to me, the homage of glances
was withdrawn, and I became an invisible woman. The comeli-
ness of my face had depended on moulding rather than sculp-
ture, and the deterioration of the outer casing quickly revealed
the weakness of the frame. Becoming pendant, on the lower
rim of this frame, was the scalloping jawline foretold ten years
before by Colin Porteous, but time's chief offence was against

my eyes. They had been wide and shallowly set, with clean-cut lids, the Australian eye adapted early to light, and I asked myself what heavy ancestral hand had set itself across my forehead, and pressed down until my brows descended on my eyelids, and two folds of flesh over the outer corners gave me the small blue triangular eyes, with the two little flax-tufted lumps of brow, that I saw so often in England.

Family accusations of selfishness and frivolity, so deeply embedded, so true, added guilt to my depression, as did the fading echo of that wartime injunction on alarm and despondency. I fought hard against the encroaching greyness. I spoke with enthusiasm of my return to Sydney, I booked my passage, bought luggage and shoes, and gathered information with apparent eagerness from Australians I met.

I was warned of the housing shortage in Sydney. 'You have a flat here,' I was told. 'You'll find it hard to get anything there.'

But I would not be deterred. If it was hard, so much the better, the less time I would have to think.

I was making a suit, for the last time, for a regular customer, a company secretary. 'How well you look,' I said. 'Have you been away?'

'Yes,' she said, 'to have my face lifted. It wasn't a matter of vanity. I'm a professional woman. I regard my face as part of my equipment. So why not keep it in the best possible condition?'

Hilda and I met for the first time in the washroom of the hospital. She was drying her hands, I was washing mine, and in the mirror we each examined the other's bandaged face through eyes surrounded by bruised and swollen flesh.

She said, 'Makes you think you've made a mistake, doesn't it?'

'I have made a mistake,' I said.

Our voices were blurred. We couldn't open our mouths very wide. 'Why?' said Hilda. 'What makes you think so?'

'I don't quite know.'

'Then don't be silly.'

'It's an intuition.'

'My intuition's usually wrong.'

'So is mine. It's only that as I was going under the anaes-thetic, I thought, "This is wrong." And it seemed so . . .'

'So definite.'

'Yes. I can't get it out of my head.'

'But it's nonsense all the same. I would laugh if I could. I am laughing. Take my laugh on trust.'

A few days later I met her again. 'I'm sorry about the other day,' I said.

'Why?'

'I might have depressed you.'

'You didn't depress *me*. I know so many people who've been done by this man.'

She was a comfort, with her stories of the marvellous trans-formations of her friends, most of whom, like Hilda herself, were actresses.

We visited each other's rooms. 'One good thing the rotten war did,' she said, 'it improved that type of surgery. What made you have yours?'

'Professional reasons.'

'Exactly!'

I told her about going back to Sydney and starting afresh. 'And I feel I can't afford to look old.'

'Exactly! You've seen my "before" photographs. What an old fright! What parts could I have got looking like that?'

But without a pause she went on. 'But of course I could have got more parts. I would have had a genuine range, middle-aged to oldish. And with television coming on, the more genuine the range the better.'

'Then why . . .'

'Vanity.'

She was looking at me sideways. 'Yes,' I agreed with relief, 'vanity.'

I became more cheerful, but, as if we were on a see-saw, the loss of my weight of worry sent Hilda's side sinking down. She was forty-seven, and had a lover of thirty. He was playing in New York, and as soon as she knew he was to go, she had made arrangements to have a facelift while he was away.

'So that I can surprise him,' she said, swinging a foot, 'with my bloody beauty.'

But now she woke in the middle of the night, and asked herself what he was doing, at that very minute in New York, and if he would ever come back at all. It would be better, she said, if he didn't. Since she was going to lose him anyway, *for certain*, it would be better if she lost him now, and got it over with.

In the middle of the night, she also thought about her son.

'I don't think it's unreasonable to want to know where he is. I haven't heard from him, let alone seen him, for five-and-a-half months. Of course I know he *will* turn up. He'll turn up when he wants money. I've never said that to anyone before. Oh, he's a charmer, an absolute charmer. I wouldn't mind a drink. I wonder if it really makes the tissues bleed. Better not risk it. Damn. I'll be glad to get out of here. It does me no good, all this time to think.'

She had been 'done' before me, so her bandages came off first. And immediately, up went her side of the see-saw.

'There! What did I tell you? He's marvellous, this man. Of course the swelling hasn't gone down yet. And those little scars, there and there, I'll cover those with my hair. I can't have my hair dyed for three weeks, but what I'll do, I'll go into hiding for three weeks, and clean out cupboards and read good books. Give me your address, and we'll have dinner or something before you go back to Sydney. I'm dying to see yours.'

As soon as she went, my side of the see-saw began to sink. The bandages came off three days later.

'There!' said the surgeon. 'Now, what did I tell you?'

It did not help that I could guess, by the strain in his voice, something of what he was feeling. It did not help that I could understand and even sympathize with him. Even the most skilled and conscientious craftsman—like him, like me—is fallible, and has, every now and again, a moment of irretrievable error. I knew that well. Couldn't I recall occasions when I had circled a customer, saying that all it needed was a bit taken in here, and a good pressing there?

'Of course,' he was saying, 'time ... the swelling ... the tightness. It does take time.'

('Of course, when the skirt has had time to hang.')

'And,' he said, 'you're not used to it yet.'

('Don't forget it's a style you've not worn before.')

The difference was that my agitated circling always ended in my confessing my liability and making what reparation was asked. 'Yes, you're right. Take it off. I'll make you another, or reimburse you, whichever you want.' But how could he admit liability? To do so would be to lay himself open to ruin. In his place I should have acted in the same way.

'As a usual thing,' he said casually, 'the benefit lasts for about five years.'

I nodded at myself in the hand mirror. Five years. Quite. Precisely. After all, I had known it would turn out like this.

'Very nice,' I said.

He gave me a sharp glance, but it was easy, with a face like that, to hide what I was thinking.

'It will be very nice,' he said constrainedly, 'in a week or so.'

'I'm sure it will be.'

I was almost purring. I was thinking that the operation had been my last throw of the dice. I had never intended going back to Sydney; I had not had the heart nor the strength. As soon as I got back to my flat, I would take all the sleeping pills I had. I wondered if there were enough. In my mind's eye, I saw the bottle, almost full. I put down the mirror.

'Thank you,' I said, softly and politely.

It did not seem worth reading the small pile of letters I found on the carpet inside my door. I crumpled them up, threw them in the grate, and as they were burning went to my bedside table and counted the pills. They say it is rare for a suicide to leave no note. I left none. I couldn't be bothered. That is the literal truth. As if influenced by my face, I was fixed in indifference. My hand did not shake nor my heart beat faster. Hand and heart were simply and equally part of the mechanism. If workmen in the street had not asked that all taps in the house be turned off, it is reasonable to suppose that I shouldn't be here now, sitting in this sun. Saved by the London County Council and a stomach pump.

Three weeks later, Hilda came to see me. I had just come home from the hospital, where I had insisted that I took the pills by accident. They didn't believe me, of course, and sent people to talk to me, but I shut my eyes and repeated the story. 'You seem to hate us for trying to help you,' said one of them. 'Not at all,' I replied. What I hated them for was the stomach pump. 'I took them by accident,' I kept saying. My face was a help. With my eyes shut, they might as well have been talking to a stone, and in the end, they went away. I should have been home in a few days except for my old enemy, bronchitis, which this time they treated with a much improved variety of the new drugs.

When Hilda came to see me I told her about the bronchitis, but made no mention of the pills because I intended to take another dose, and did not want her to feel that she could have stopped me if she had said this, or done that. She had had her hair dyed, and set so that it concealed her scars, and when she had come in, wearing a new suit, and a hat with a little veil, she had had an air of responsiveness to the early Spring day, or to anything else that might turn up. All this had vanished at the sight of my face, but she quickly controlled her dismay and began to chatter, to tell me that her son had turned up, and her lover was due next week. She could not keep it up, however. She suddenly stopped. '*Oh, Nora!*' she said, and sat on the edge of my bed.

Misfortune impressed her. She reminded me of Olive in the abortionist's waiting room. I waved a hand. 'I'm laughing,' I said. 'Take my laughter on trust.'

'Oh, but it *will* be all right.'

But I would not discuss it. I sat down and told her about the new drugs for bronchitis, and every time she tried to interrupt, I told her a bit more.

'Another benefit of the war. It seems,' I said, amused by the double meaning private to myself, 'that I shall never again have such terrible bronchitis.'

'That's wonderful,' she said unhappily.

'Isn't it! Not even in a cold winter.'

'But are Sydney winters so cold?'

'Oh, I've changed my mind. I'm not going back.'

'Why not?'

'They say the housing shortage is terrible there. The population has doubled, or some such thing. And after all, I *have* a flat here.'

'And will you still make clothes?'

'I don't know yet.'

She went to my mirror and twitched at the veil of her hat. 'Do you like my hat? I got it from a little lady who has come up from the country to open a hat shop. Poor darling, she's going broke.'

But her worried eyes were watching me in the mirror. 'What about that dinner we were going to have?'

I pressed a hand to my chest. 'I'm still a bit ...'

'Well, I'll ring you.'

I smiled at her. Between us were a few feet of space, and (again) the great distance created by my intentions. 'All right,' I said, 'do that. Say, the end of next week.'

The pills I had taken had sent me away so easily, first heaving me up on the swell of a wave, and then dropping and engulfing me, that I did not want to use any other kind. The process had not been so *entirely* pleasant that I could not imagine horror, during that drop and final engulfment, if the method should differ even slightly. But I had none of the pills left, and after what had happened I could hardly go back to my usual doctor and ask for more, and the fraud and finagling by which I intended to get them would take about a week.

Before the end of that week Hilda came back.

'Nora, do you want a job?'

Amusement would have aroused her suspicions. 'What kind of a job?'

'At a theatrical costumers. I've just heard of it.'

'I'm not interested in theatrical costumes, Hilda.'

'Yes, you are.'

'I don't know what makes you think so.'

'The way you spoke of Gischia's designs for *Murder*.'

She meant *Murder in the Cathedral*. 'I'm not a designer,' I said.

'I know you're not. I'm talking about making. Try it, Nora. I know the people.'

'It's much too specialized.'

But even as I shook my head, my interior eye was assailed by a medley of rich rippling colour, of bright lights and inhabited shadow—all latterly derived from the theatre, no doubt, but

first of all from Ida Mayo's hands manipulating satins and bro-
cades beneath her little lamps.

Hilda was watching me. 'They badly need someone,' she
murmured.

'If I can get it,' I said, 'I'll take it.'

I got the job and the pills on the same day. I put the pills
in my bedside drawer, and with the relief of death available at
my right hand, so to speak, I decided to hang on, provisionally, from day to day. 'Provisionally' was the word always in my
mind. Before a week was out it was clear that I had fallen among
people who would accept me for what I was, whatever I was,
and in that same week, the work itself began to engross me. Far
from being a drastic departure from my former work, I found it
an illumination and a synthesis of it. Those women 'mad about
clothes', always running to me with bits of cloth and pictures cut
from magazines, always asking 'But is it *me*?' hadn't they been
forever seeking to express their conception of themselves? And
wasn't that conception usually imaginary? A composed character? I myself had once dressed with the same vague intention.

Vague. Yes. One impediment to success was the vagueness
of the intention. Like most amateurs, they, and I, were beset
and confused by vogues imposed from outside, by persons who
seemed as unstable and capricious as ourselves. For that reason,
success was discouragingly rare, but in theatrical work, where a
clear intention is carried out by a team of professionals, success
is exhilaratingly regular, though never to be taken for granted.
As for the special problems, I found them easy to surmount.
If you can make a good suit, you can make anything, and it is
not difficult to pick up the tricks that make cumbersome robes
manageable, or a garment easy and quick to put on and take off.

I became chief dressmaker, and worked with many designers. A few were brilliant, and I often had the pleasure of seeing one of these alter his designs at my suggestion, a pleasure

denied to him, since it was a natural part of his great talent that he absorbed suggestion and regarded the result as wholly his own. I did not resent it. What could have better suited my nature, as it had developed, than exerting the more influence by pretending to have none? And if I sometimes heard, in ironic echo, Una Porteous's voice bemoaning my inability to *handle* a man, and stopped to wonder, I did not really find it surprising that I was ready to develop a diplomacy, in the interest of this work, that I had refused to develop in marriage with Colin Porteous.

In a year or so, except when very tired, I stopped fussing about my face as I had once stopped fussing about my clothes, and in fact, some blessed lines had begun to reappear, and mobility to return. *That*, if you like, had been a mistake in theatrical presentation.

Though I never consciously and finally renounced my intention of returning to Australia (and was later to find the vestiges of that intention embedded in me), I no longer spoke of it, and I suppose that it was at this time that my memories of my home country began to grow blurred and misshapen. Holland Park was my village, my flat, my resting place, but how eagerly, after the idleness of Sunday, I returned to my work. I grew to love those big cluttered low-ceilinged rooms, and the memory of winter afternoons there—the light, the smell, the visitors and the voices—can still fill me with nostalgia. I worked there, always a subordinate to the designers, for twelve full years, and as a part-time overseer for another six. I sometimes think I would still be there but for my hands, and, to a lesser extent, my eyes. They let me down badly, those two.

The warmth is making me drowsy. I let Dorothy Rainbow's embroidery drop to the floor and fold my hands in my lap. In this spring sunshine I have my first unqualified pleasure in being back. I reflect that it was worth hanging on, provisionally, if only for this present blessing of sun on the skin. I ask myself why Dorothy Rainbow did not hang on, provisionally, and why nothing was offered to appease the remnants of that need that once drove her to walk. I think of how the web of her tracks across the suburb must have merged with the web of mine, and how in dry weather we both trod in little puffs of dust and left low cumulus trails behind us. She wears narrow black boots and treads in this dust absently and gently, her head nodding as if to a tune audible only to her. Her son also has a preoccupied air, but if he gives the effect of hearing music, it is a heavy and solemn music ...

I open my eyes and stare at the wall. The evasiveness of the Custs, the dust on the magpie embroidery, and Grace's comment—'*The Rainbow house is up for sale ...*' combine in my mind to form an incredible pattern. Oh, but surely, an incredible pattern. To disperse it, to smash it by movement, I pick up the magpie embroidery and take it to the window.

Here, from another angle than on that first day, is the lawn, the cabbage-tree palm, the street. I shake the embroidery out of the window, releasing much dust, and then stand and stare, like Lyn Wilmot or Una Porteous, up and down the street. A little girl opens a garden gate and steps into the street, while from the other direction comes an old gentleman, very tall, thin, sallow, and all in white, Don Quixote dressed for bowls. They meet. He pulls his rag hat from his head, extends one foot, and bows very low. The little girl and I laugh at the same time. They cross and part, drawing further and further away from each other on the street, and I look longingly from one to the other until both disappear. I don't go back to the chair. Even in winter and early spring the sun here is never as gentle as it seems at first. It has made me slightly sick. I go back to bed and in less than a minute I am asleep.

'Nora. Nora.'

Betty Cust's voice, very low, is testing the depth of my sleep. I want her to go away, but the recollection of all her kindness obliges me to open my eyes.

'I've brought you two letters.'

They are from Hilda and Liza. I am too excited to find my spectacles. I pull open the bedside drawer, I give anxious cries and thump the bedclothes. It is Betty who finds them. She takes them from the back of the drawer and gives them to me.

I read bits of the letters aloud, and then put them aside to read carefully and privately later. I sit back and beam at Betty. How truly incredible my incredible pattern seems now, a product of sickness and loneliness. Smiling at my joy, Betty takes my place in the cane chair, with her sun-spotted hands folded in her lap, and asks if either Hilda or Liza had children. I speak vaguely of Hilda's son, being dubious about explaining the breach between them when he 'got off' with her lover, but I can be quite frank about Liza, who in the war years suffered such drastic bereavement, losing her husband and all three of her sons.

I am sociable and talkative. I describe Liza's hat shop and how Hilda and I tried to stave off her ruin by sending people to buy her hats.

'But it was hopeless. She had always wanted a hat shop in London, and she didn't even notice that young people weren't wearing hats any more. It was through her that we met Fred. He was looking for tenants for the two top floors of his house. They had been vacant for years because his requirements were so particular. He wanted three thin old women.'

'Why thin?'

'He couldn't bear fat women.'

Thin Betty, on behalf of all fat women, is offended. 'Too bad about him!'

'That's exactly what we used to tell him.'

'He sounds quite unreasonable.'

'Oh, poor dear, he was. Is, I mean. He's not dead.'

'Was that the house where Peter visited you, the last time he went over?'

'Yes. On Lansdowne Rise, not far from where he visited me the first time, when I was still in Holland Park. All the little back gardens in that block opened on to a private square. What we liked about the square was that it was *hilly*. Some of it was mown grass, but there were patches of old elms and beeches and broken paving and shrubs gone wild. If you stood under one of those big trees you could imagine yourself in a forest. Or if you were feeling urban you could sit out in the open, on one of the benches, and see people at the back windows of the houses. The houses were all the same, of course, three stories with cellars . . .'

I go on to describe Fred's house, but as I speak I see the four of us in the square on a summer evening. We are all sitting on one bench, Fred sideways on an end, when Liza says, 'Look.' We look where she is pointing and see that Belle, having missed us, has extended her head round the garden gate. She sees us, comes through the gate, sits down and licks herself, and then sets out towards us at her leisure. The sunlight seems infused with a blueish smoke, though no fires are burning, and we all watch Belle stepping with deliberation across the grass, through shade and then through smoky sunlight, until, knowing herself observed, she sits down and cleans herself again. We all look away, pretending indifference, and presently she comes on again, with no sign of pleasure or recognition or even of her real intention, until she arrives at our feet. She then composedly sits, with her back to us, and we all relax, and look at the sky, and into the trees and the smoky light, and begin to talk in quiet voices.

I am still describing the house to Betty, and now I say, as the twilight dulls and we rise reluctantly from the bench, 'It wasn't a house from the best period. The hall was rather narrow and the moulding wasn't good. But it was pleasant. It was one of those pleasant houses.'

'Peter told us about it.'

I know by her tone that he has disparaged it. 'It wasn't to Peter's taste,' I say. 'He said it had a funny smell. And he was right, you know. We used to notice it ourselves whenever we came back from the country. But then we got used to it all over again, and forgot all about it. I think it came from the cellar. Fred used to keep his wine there, but Hilda and Liza and I wouldn't go near the place, because of the rats.'

'Rats! Not really! Heavens, Nora, no wonder your friends are so happy to be out of it.'

'They're happy to have got a cheap flat.'

But the apparent happiness of Hilda and Liza is, in fact, what makes me read their letters with such care after Betty goes. I read Hilda's first, alert for the word, the note, by which she might betray herself. I don't find it, and conclude that she is as cheerful as she sounds. I am not so certain about Liza, whose cheerfulness, on examination, gives a slightly wild, shrugging effect. She is less robust and adaptable than Hilda, and besides, of the three of us, she suffered most from the break because Fred had been for her, for so long, a kind of Lewie. When her husband was still alive, Fred was her neighbour in Surrey. His grandmother, who had brought him up, had died by that time, but not before she had implanted in Fred a fear that every woman who said a friendly word to him was 'after him'. In consequence, all his friends were young men or old women. Liza was a special case. She was a neighbour, she was very thin, her happy marriage was a safeguard, and of course, she was 'simpatica'. Even so, he would have his jumpy spells when alone with her, and Liza said she ought to have known better than to say what she did. Her husband had begun a long period at home, with a fractured knee, just as Liza had begun to redecorate the house, and one day she said to Fred, 'Oh, the things I shall do when I get rid of Theo!'

'I wish you could have seen him,' she would tell us. 'He gave a great equine quiver and ran away and hid himself for a month. No, really, a whole month. All I ever saw of him all that time was his hat gliding at great speed along the top of the hedge. I think he bought roller skates. I didn't know what to do. I couldn't go and knock at his door. He would have run and hidden under a bed. And as for writing a little note! No, I could only do it in words, face to face. I almost caught him a number of times in the village, but he always saw me coming and managed to escape. But at last I caught him in the doorway of a shop. It was a narrow doorway, a real ambush. He raised his hat and tried to dodge past me, but I caught his sleeve, and that made him stop, because there were people around who knew us both. So he stopped, and I said, 'Oh, you silly man. All I meant was that I was waiting for Theo to go back to work, so that I could get on with the house.'

Very gradually, they became friends again, though Liza swore he never quite got over it. 'It's no good. He suspects me to this day.'

Most of this she would say in his presence, and sometimes, when we were all together, and a silence had fallen, she would look at him and say, very quietly, 'Look out, Fred.' And Fred would hiss and duck his head and splutter with laughter. 'That's all very well,' he would say, 'but I don't trust any of you. Just as well there are three of you. Safety in numbers.'

None of us foresaw that this farcical mistrust would end by wrecking our association. One day Fred rubbed his chin and frowned.

'I don't trust that Australian,' he said.

We all looked at him. 'What Australian?' asked Hilda.

But Fred was still rubbing his chin. 'And that nephew of hers, that Peter Chiddy, the day he came here he stole two of my books.'

He went out of the room. We all looked at each other. 'What do you make of that?' asked Hilda in a hushed voice.

Liza bent her head and set her fingertips on her forehead. 'I don't know what to make of it.'

The next day Fred accused the milkman of cheating, and attacked him with his stick. The man was not hurt, and nothing came of it, but through the house worry and trepidation spread. For three days we saw nothing of him, though we could hear him moving about in his flat on the ground floor. On the third day he came into Liza's sitting room without knocking. We were all there. He looked and sounded calm and businesslike.

'Someone has been drinking my burgundy,' he said. 'The stuff closest to the door. I know who it was. It was that Australian.'

'Oh, Fred dear,' said Liza, 'don't be silly.'

'I think you had better keep quiet, Liza. We all know what you're after.'

In nervous response to this old joke, Hilda laughed. Fred went wild.

'Bloody women!' he shouted. 'With your great bloody tits!'

We all sat perfectly still. Fred went out, muttering and tumbling over his feet. 'Did anyone see where I put my spectacles?' asked Liza in a dazed voice, and Hilda said briskly, 'Yes, over there by the clock.'

Fred did not return to the house that night, nor the next.

'Hadn't we better get in touch with his sister?' I asked.

'I daren't,' said Liza. 'You know how he hates her.'

'Hers are bigger than any of ours,' said Hilda.

'Oh, Hilda,' said Liza sadly.

'Sorry,' said Hilda.

'I think we should ring Mr Pope,' said Liza.

Mr Pope was Fred's lawyer. 'Don't worry,' he said. 'I know where he is. You will hear in due course.'

'You see?' I said.

'No,' said Liza, 'I don't.'

'Due course,' said Hilda. 'I never know what that means.'

I reminded them that Fred had gone away without notice the year before. 'And he was only in Cornwall.'

But Hilda said, 'What will happen if he has gone mad and violent?'

'He will have to be put away,' said Liza.

'No, I mean,' said Hilda, 'what will happen to us?'

None of us wanted to think about it. The lease of the house was Fred's, and in spite of rises in costs, our rents had not changed since we had moved in ten years before, at a time when all our incomes had begun to wither. Fred had been our friend and benefactor, and in our worry for him we were mortified by our worry for ourselves.

At last his sister rang. Fred had been arrested for belabouring a bus conductor and was now in a mental hospital. A few days later she appeared at number six.

'No, I'm sorry, no one can see him. He wouldn't know you, in any case. He's in a very good place, getting the best possible care, but they don't hold out any hope of recovery. Not this time. It's the place he went to last May.'

'But last May he went to Cornwall.'

'Is that what he told you?'

She had been given legal power to act for him. She remarked that our arrangement with him seemed to have been very personal and casual. 'Mr Pope says no records were kept. What exactly were you paying him?'

She nodded when we told her. 'That's what Fred told Mr

Pope, but I simply couldn't believe it. Well, I'm very sorry, but that's all over now. This house must be made to pay its way. Fred's expenses are enormous.'

None of us could even begin to pay the rents she had decided on.

'I'm very sorry, but this is the welfare state, after all. We taxpayers can hardly be expected to pay individually as well.'

None of us could refute this argument.

'And I know you would not want to deprive Fred of the best possible care.'

So it was necessary to look at once for a flat.

'We will need three bedrooms,' said Liza.

'Of course,' said Hilda. 'But we won't be silly, and look in Kensington.'

'There are parts of West Kensington,' said Liza vaguely.

'Maida Vale used to be cheap,' I said.

'I don't think it is now,' said Hilda. 'But there *was* a part of South Hampstead, over near Kilburn.'

We knew, of course, that London had changed. Fred, who went out more often than any of us, had come home sometimes and said, 'We are positively surrounded by tatt and chaos, but so far, so far, we're safe here.' And it was the safety of our sanctuary that had prevented us from *feeling* the change, instead of merely knowing of it. We were still able to believe that 'London is made up of villages. Here we all live in our own little village.' But when we went out into London, without our sanctuary at our backs, when we went out into London and exposed our needs to it, we realized that all those villages were now meshed by the flow of traffic into one huge hard city, whose constant movement confused us, and whose noise beat upon our brains.

And of course we knew, too, that rents had gone up. But *our* rents had not gone up. Again, our knowledge had not been personal. And impersonal knowledge has not much cutting edge.

We sat in cafés, our slipped shoes under the table.

'Imagine asking fifty for that grisly place,' I said.

'I bet Crippen lived there,' said Hilda. 'Come to think of it, wasn't there a plaque?'

'I think there was,' I said, 'But even so, it was better than that one at sixty.'

Liza stirred her tea without a smile. 'I'm sick of the whole thing.'

When we got home on the third day, we found Fred's sister in the hall, with a man.

'I'm very sorry to intrude, but Mr Parker must see the house if he's to sell the lease. Have you found anything yet?'

We said we hadn't.

'Well, I don't want to hurry you. A week's notice is the usual thing, but I'm sure Fred would want you to have a fortnight. That's eleven more days, isn't it? There was a cat in here, by the way. I put him out of the back door.'

'Her,' said Hilda.

'I beg your pardon.'

'She's a female.'

'Oh, is she? Well, you'll find her out in the square. Perhaps you would like to wait there, too, until Mr Parker has looked at the house.'

In the square we sat on a bench facing the house. Belle sat sedately at our feet.

'We could do with two bedrooms,' I said, 'if one of us used the sitting room as a bedroom.'

'And the other two walked through it to get to the kitchen,' said Liza.

'It would depend on the layout,' I agreed.

'*And* you wouldn't get it for less than forty,' said Hilda.

'I can't go on with this,' said Liza quietly.

Hilda and I pretended not to hear. We all watched as Fred's

sister and Mr Parker, at a downstairs window, examined the marks of Belle's claws on the sill.

'There's my sister in Coventry,' said Hilda.

We had already heard about Hilda's sister in Coventry. A few years ago she and her husband had subdivided their house. A few weeks ago they had lost their tenants.

'But we've decided not to leave London,' I said.

'What does it matter if we do?' said Liza.

She had bent to loosen her shoelaces, to ease her swollen feet. Hilda and I exchanged glances across her back.

'Well, nowadays it does *seem*,' said Hilda carefully, 'that the charm of London depends on how much *money* one has.'

'Let us try London for one last day,' I said.

'Do you mind if I don't come?' said Liza.

Hilda and I set out early next morning. Released from the weight of Liza's apathy, we sprang away confident and even gay. The day was windy and slightly rainy. 'Refreshing,' we said, putting up our umbrellas. When the rain increased we made no comment on it, nor on our wet shoes and stockings, but as we stood waiting for the bus to take us to our third flat, we stopped speaking and anxiously craned our heads out of the queue. While walking along strange streets, following directions given us, we spoke only to ask each other how much further, or could we possibly have missed the turning.

At about three o'clock Hilda said, 'I must go to the loo.'

It was now raining heavily. 'Can't you wait till we get to this flat?'

'Absolutely not.' She showed me her road guide. 'Look, it's way up there.'

'Then we'll go to the nearest underground.'

Willesden Green was the nearest, though it took us away from our destination. As Hilda was washing her hands, I consulted a road map and a map of the underground.

'Instead of retracing our steps in this rain, we could go by underground to North Wembley.'

She came and looked over my shoulder. 'We would have to change at Baker Street, and from North Wembley it's still a fair walk.'

'We could get a cab.'

'A cab?'

'Just this once.'

'A *cab*! Yes, let's *do* that. Let's get a cab from here to number six.'

What a relief it was to give in, to become passive, simply to accept whatever might happen. That first stage of our passivity was not sad like Liza's, but childish and gay. In the taxi we chatted and laughed like schoolgirls.

It was fine next day when we all went to Coventry. Hilda's sister and brother-in-law stood together in the doorway and greeted us as we crossed the strip of garden that separated their neat gabled house from the street. Together they conducted us over the empty first floor.

'There are only two bedrooms, but the big one could be partitioned off down the middle.'

'Of course it could,' said Hilda.

'Yes,' said Liza.

I said nothing. From the window I could see the rectilinear pattern made by straight streets and a hundred neat roofs. Iron-grey and terracotta. Who would have thought that at my age I could feel it again—the old oppression, the breast breaker?

'And we've got the colour television downstairs. Haven't we, Tom? And we're always glad of company. And there's a fair-sized garden at the back you can have the run of. We're letting the place cheap because after the last lot we had we've got to know who we're getting. There's only one thing. No cats. Tom's allergic.'

Tom took his pipe out of his mouth. 'Doctor's orders.'

We conferred in the train on the way up to London. 'It's cheap,' said Hilda. 'It's not poky. And it's really not far from London. We could go up quite often. What do you think, Liza?'

Liza's little headshake was not in rejection, but in unwillingness to be aroused from her inertia. 'I just want to get it over.'

Hilda looked at me. 'Nora?'

'It would mean getting a new owner for Belle.'

'That will be easy. Belle's so charming. We could manage very well, with the rent cut three ways.'

'Could you still manage if you cut it two ways?'

'For two I'm sure she would make it less. Why?'

Liza had shut her eyes. 'Because Nora's going back to Australia,' she said.

'If only we had more time,' I said.

That night, Fred's sister rang again, 'It isn't that I want to hurry you ...'

Again we conferred. 'As far as I'm concerned,' said Hilda, 'that's *it*. I'm sick of the whole thing.'

'I don't care where we go,' said Liza, 'as long as we get out of here.'

My heart gave an unexpected leap. 'I've decided to go back,' I said. 'I will sell all my furniture, my china and glass, even my Persian rug. I'll go back with two suitcases of clothes, and my books can follow me by ship.'

Energy infused me as I spoke. Many years before I had come to London because I was entranced by the knowledge that *nobody could stop me*. Did I return because I was in need of the energy generated by an equally drastic decision? Hilda and Liza looked at me for a while in silence.

'You will be warm, anyway,' said Hilda then.

'And safe,' said Liza.

In spring Belle usually spent much time in the square, her doings watched and commented on by us from our windows. But that last week, as we packed, she spent her days pacing from room to room. If one of us bent and extended a hand, she would approach, but would then turn aside just short of it and rub her head, from cheek to cranium, against a table leg, or she would caress a door frame with her flank. Nobody wanted her. We advertised, we canvassed acquaintances, we knocked on all the doors in the square, and even on doors in other squares, and asked if anyone would take a cat. We came home, shaking our heads, while Belle, in the hall, rubbed her head repeatedly against the umbrella stand.

When she was given to us she was already spayed, so no unpleasant decisions had had to be made. It was Liza who voiced this one.

'She will have to be put down.'

'You sound as if you don't care,' said Hilda.

Liza flared suddenly, shockingly, into life. 'I have protested at too many hard fates. I can protest no more.' Though her eyes were dry and angry, her voice was hoarse as if from weeping. '*No more!*'

As soon as Hilda and I were alone, I said, 'If anything happens to impede these plans, Liza will crack up.'

'Yes. It's Liza or Belle. But *God*,' said Hilda, '*I* can still protest.' She took a handkerchief from her pocket, wiped her eyes, and blew her nose. 'But,' she said then, 'that's all I can do.'

The vet came twice with a cage, but neither time could Belle be found. 'I'll have to leave it with you ladies,' he said. 'You put her in, and I'll collect it.' Hilda and I meant to put her in together, but on the appointed day, the vet rang to postpone his call, so that it was I, the last to leave the house, who put her in the cage.

Neither Hilda nor Liza mentioned Belle in her letter. They are being 'sensible' about it. I shall be equally 'sensible' and not mention her when I reply.

A well-sprung mattress, a modern kitchen, an efficient hot water service. How glad I am that Grace made these concessions to the times. I have had the first before, but never the last two. In the morning I have a bath, long, deep, and forbidden, then put on a warm dressing gown and slippers and go to the kitchen.

The small pawpaw sent by Arch Cust has arrived at perfect ripeness and infuses the kitchen with its scent. A transverse sun entering the window has flung a lozenge of light on to the table. I carry the pawpaw, on its white plate, and set it down in this light. Memories of Arch make me handle it with a sort of humorous ritual. With deliberation and enjoyment, I shall eat it.

I cut it in two lengthwise, scoop out the shining black seeds, and bring the first spoonful to my mouth. Without a doubt, it is the most delicious fruit in the world, but like certain little jokes, it ought to be consumed only where it grows. At number six I once described the procreating methods of the male and female trees. How fascinated Fred was. I think he felt it should always be done in that way.

As my spoon cuts close to the skin (which I am trying, as in childhood, not to break), Lyn Wilmot comes into the kitchen with my pint of milk. She gives a shriek when she sees me.

'*Should you be here?*'

'Why not? I'm allowed to get up.'

'He said only in a chair.'

'I am in a chair.'

'He didn't say that kind of chair.'

And now she wants to bustle me back to bed and wait on

me, just as Una Porteous, after I had signed everything and was packing my suitcase, wanted to kiss me and bemoan with me the 'tragedy' of divorce.

I remember to be meek. 'Doctor Rainbow does let me go to the bathroom.'

'Oh, does he? I didn't know.'

'But if you really think I shouldn't be here ...'

'Oh no, I suppose it's all right. He must know what he's doing. Just because I like Doctor Smith best doesn't mean I think Doctor Rainbow's no good. His manner puts me off, that's what it is. Gives me the creeps. But to be honest, I don't know if it's really his manner, or knowing about his mother committing all those murders.'

I nod without looking up from my pawpaw. My pattern of yesterday was credible after all, but if horrors are to be recounted, I prefer to hear them from Betty or Jack Cust. I fold the unbroken pawpaw skin (as in childhood) like cloth. 'I wonder if pawpaw is bad for arthritis,' I say, as I carry the plate to the kitchen bin. 'I do hope not.'

I go back to bed. The story of Dorothy Rainbow's fate having progressed from accident to suicide, and from simple suicide to suicide with murder, it is understandable that by the time Betty Cust arrives my imagination should have supplied a choice of further progressions, so that Betty's story of the axe, and of Dorothy's husband and all her children but one, Gordon, killed in their beds, does not really surprise me. One has read of such things. As Betty speaks, she stands as if toeing a line, with both hands pressed to her cheeks and her eyebrows squirming as if in a recreation of bewilderment.

'There was only Gordon. He woke up and saw her, and ran away and hid under the house. There was a big old packing case there, a piano case. The children used to use it for a cubby. He curled up in a corner and pulled cloth and papers over his head.

He told them he heard her moving about looking for him, but in the end she went off again. Then he heard her in the house, and after a while everything was quiet, so he crept out and crept back upstairs. But when he saw all the others, and her with her head in the gas oven, he ran off again. They found him the next morning, trying to catch yabbies in an old jam tin in the creek behind the school. They asked him why he hadn't run for the police, but he was only eight.'

'Could anyone else have been saved if he had?'

'No. Only her.'

'Poor child.'

'Oh, yes!'

I have heard the story, I have accepted the facts, so why should shock come now like a wall collapsing. 'But,' I say, '*an axe!*'

'Nora, I know. None of us ever, ever, understood how she could do it.'

I feel the imminence of an angry speech. 'If one of you had, she may not have done it.' I am glad I suppressed it. What reason have I to suppose that anyone could have stemmed a tide of that sort?

'She was so gentle,' says Betty.

'She was anxious to please, I remember that. She can't have been gentle.'

'Gentle when she was her true self.'

'Perhaps when she was one of her true selves. But how many selves did she have? And how many of those selves did her life call upon? We can only know this—one of them was not gentle.'

'That one never showed. Truly, Nora, never. She did have a sort of a breakdown just before the war. But nothing violent. Only refusing to leave the house, and hiding when anyone knocked. You know the kind of thing?'

'Yes,' I say. 'I know the kind of thing.'

'Nowadays they call it suburban neurosis. But in those days there were plenty of people who said she needed a good slap, or that she ought to have something real to worry about. Still, others recognised it as a sickness, and she did have treatment, sedatives and things. She always said it was Grace who pulled her out of it in the end. When the war started Grace took her to the Red Cross, and wouldn't let her give up when she wanted to. And she did get to love it, Nora. Truly. I've never known anyone work so hard. She was tireless.'

I find nothing to say that can be said. Betty gets my breakfast, but I can't eat it. 'I am so cross with Lyn Wilmot,' she says. She attributes my fatigue and lack of appetite to the revelation of Dorothy Rainbow's tragic end. She does not know, of course, about my rashness in having had that long bath.

It is Saturday, and after Betty goes I lie and wonder if noises sound so clear and isolated because it is not a working day, or because I know it is not a working day. I move my lips and hear myself say again, 'But *an axe*!' And this time I recognise that part of my shock was caused by the ugly grisly method. Poison or bullets, equally deadly and perhaps slower, would not have shocked me so much. The axe is an offence, evidently, against the aesthetics of murder. Though disgusted by this evidence of my own wincing 'good taste', I am not surprised. For a long time I have been critical of this one of my many selves, this sickly and over-fastidious creature, and indeed I have often wondered what effect it has had on my life. And though by my awareness of it I have possibly been saved from its worst excesses, I always conclude that its effect has been bad, almost entirely bad.

I fall asleep and am awakened by Doctor Rainbow, to whom Saturday makes no difference at all.

'Let's have a look at you.' He is already doing so. 'Breathe. Good. Again. Yes, that's fine. Now, this side. Breathe . . .'

He puts a thermometer under my arm, looks at his watch, then stands with his arms folded and waits. I watch his face, and compose a speech I will not make.

'What were you thinking of as you watched the yabbies rising in the water and listened to the soughing of the she-oaks? Or had thought been shocked to a standstill? You were eight. Did you know that gas was lethal?'

I am still watching his face as he reads the thermometer. 'Good. That's very good. You may get up for longer today.'

He is really pleased. I am astonished that the slight recovery of one old woman could mean anything to him. It is a pity to disappoint him.

'I don't want to get up at all.'

'Why not?'

'I am too tired.'

'Oh, come along. This won't do.'

'I'm sorry. I'm afraid it will have to do. I must sleep.'

He is disapproving but silent. What can he do? After he goes I lie on my side and pull the bedclothes over my ears. I hear Jack Cust come into the house, and, a little later, Betty, but on both occasions I pretend I am asleep. I think Doctor Rainbow must have told them I am being 'difficult'. Yes, in this somnolent Saturday afternoon, I think I have made a tiny, meaningless flurry. I am sick with boredom at the thought of it.

Again I hear the distant rifle fire, so like that other thud, of tennis balls against the taut-sprung racquet. I lie on my side, with my head drawn into my shoulders. I am uncomfortable, yet resistant to movement, hungry, yet resistant to food. Betty Cust comes again, and this time, in case she should be alarmed enough to call Doctor Rainbow, I force myself to roll over and open my eyes.

'Still not hungry, Nora?'

'I want nothing.'

She has brought me Mrs Partridge's embroidery. With cold politeness, I sit up and let her spread it on my lap. I look at it for a few minutes, then say flatly, almost sullenly, 'It is very good.'

'Isn't it! Though the maggie's still my favourite.'

So it may be, but this one is by far the best of the three. It is truly amazing. I swear that with my swirling suns, moons, and stars, I forestalled Lurçat. It was one of those I sat up to work on until the early hours of the morning, so that next day I dozed in the stock room of the shop in town. Its excellence disturbs as well as amazes me. I hold it up by the corners.

'I wonder what would have happened if I had never left this place.'

'Haven't you ever wondered before?'

'Never. Never once. I always believed it was imperative. But this shows I had begun to do something here after all. I have never done anything of this quality since. Who knows what else I may have drawn . . .'

I stop myself in time. The words in my mind were 'drawn out of the compression of a secret life'. But to say them is to be obliged to explain them, and in any case, Betty, smiling brightly, seems to consider my speculation as already complete.

'No, you can never tell about these things, can you? You know, Grace always said you would come back.'

'She was right, I did. But very very late. And like anything else I have ever done, against my intentions. I never intended to return here. Although I did once intend to return to Sydney.'

'I know. She was so disappointed when you changed your mind.'

'Disappointed? I thought she was annoyed. She had a way of being annoyed with me.'

Betty looks at me with her head first on one side, then on the other. 'Sometimes, when you talk about Grace, I feel I'm eavesdropping.'

I am rather taken aback. In my association with Betty I have tended to take it for granted that *I* am the clever one. 'Well,' I say, 'she practically stopped writing to me. Though perhaps that was because she just couldn't be bothered with anything much any more. Dorothy and she had been friends all their lives. I can well imagine how that horrible event must have made Grace sick and disgusted with everything.'

Again Betty looks at me with her head tilted. I have often veered away from a subject because I have believed that her experience cannot encompass mine, but I have never wondered until now if she sometimes has the same difficulty. Her reflective face suggests it, and so does her tone of resignation when she says, 'Nora, I'll bring some water and glucose and put it by your bed. And I've left some fish soup in the fridge, in case you're hungry later.' She smiles. 'Do try to eat it.'

I see that she wants to leave me in a cheerful mood. She picks up the embroidery, holds it at arm's length, and looks at it in a lively way.

'I think after all it *is* the best.'

She has no talent for falsity. 'There is no doubt about it,' I say snappishly.

'Well, wait till you're quite better, Nora. You'll do something just as good.'

We seem to have returned to our usual plane. Her ignorance embarrasses me. I change the subject. 'I do hope Mrs Partridge hung it among her New Guinea masks. The juxtaposition would be amusing.'

'She didn't. She likes it so much she keeps it over her writing desk. But she said to tell you to keep it if you like. Her eyesight is so bad she can't appreciate it now.'

'I should like her to have it back, all the same.'

'Then take it back yourself, Nora, when you're better.'

It is getting dark by the time she finally leaves. My hunger passes. There is no moon, and for once I wish that the house were closer to the street. The silence is stifling. I do not sleep, but turn in my bed in various attitudes of patient discomfort. I think of Dorothy Rainbow and her axe, and wonder what kind of monster I am that my thoughts should flow with such apparent naturalness from her to Belle, from the woman to the cat. I pick Belle up again (as I was bound to do), and feel again beneath my hands the flow of her blood and her strong heart beating. For she was, at first, as supine as heavy cloth, or as that ugly fur 'piece' I wore when boarding the ship for London.

Was it my own disgust I attributed to Grace? When I was young I used to respond to meaningless cruelty with tears and sullen deep rebellion, but in later years, and especially these latest years, what I feel is an intense and general disgust that quickly turns to self-disgust, a torpid and poisoned state of which I have a great dread. But tonight I offer it no resistance. I can't be bothered. I accept it. My mouth grows wry with it. I am still enveloped by it as I drop off to sleep.

But in my sleep the heavy gentle animal receives her charge of knowledge and is convulsed beneath my hands. I cry out and grip her hard. She bucks and twists, her claws strike my wrist, terror flows from her to me, and I shout with rage and cram her frantically into the cage. I am still cramming her in, pushing and shouting, and cursing her for my unbearable pity, when I wake up.

I wake up to the smell of blood. There is blood on my wrist and blood soaking my nightdress and the bed. 'Something terrible has happened,' I say to myself. 'I am bleeding. As soon as my heart stops pounding, I must open my eyes, and turn on the light, and see what has happened.'

So much blood cannot have come only from the reopened wound on my wrist, but I am careful to spare it as I move to the side of the bed and turn on the light with my right hand.

But I can no longer smell blood. Has the light dispelled it? I raise my left wrist. On the skin, crossing the blue veins, runs the taut pink line of a healed scar. I raise the sheets and see that a heavy sweat has made my nightdress stick to my skin. And—there is no doubt about it—I am extremely hungry.

I change my nightdress and am comforted by the touch of dry cloth on my skin. I am too hungry to be tempted by water and glucose. As I walk to the kitchen it seems that it is my hunger, and not the lights I turn on as I go, that presses back the darkness in my path. Betty has put an electric radiator in the kitchen. I turn it on before I take the fish soup from the refrigerator.

I have health. In my mind and my body, health persists. Not perfect health, but enough to combat the sicknesses of my mind and body.

After I have eaten and washed my dishes I go to the hall cupboard and take out two fresh sheets. Changing my bed is a laborious matter, but there is enjoyment in deploying my patience, my persistence. When the bed is made I climb into it, sighing with relief, and fall at once into a deep sleep.

I wake to the sound of lonely footsteps in the street. A single person, light-footed, is passing at a slow but not desultory pace. Then comes another. Then the sound of several cars. Then the busier broken pattering of a small group on foot. Then one car. It is scarcely light. The cars disturb a pattern that is otherwise hauntingly familiar, but it is not until all sound has died away that I hear my mother's voice.

'There go the Catholics, off to Mass.'

She always said 'Mass' with an amused inflection. So did Fred. Liza was a Catholic. 'Of the back-sliding kind,' she once said. 'Is there any other kind?' enquired Fred. 'Not one in the whole world,' replied Liza. 'But think how much further we might slide without it.'

Doctor Rainbow is not quite so unaffected by Sunday as by Saturday. He arrives about nine, wearing a crumpled tweed jacket and grey trousers instead of a crumpled suit. I come out of the bathroom to find him standing in the hall.

'You've had a bath,' he says.

'A shower,' I say. 'Is that permitted?'

'I don't recommend it. But I suppose I can't stop you. You're like your sister.'

'Were you Grace's doctor?'

'I tried to be. She was wilful, you know. She did as she pleased.' And then he adds, with his queer stiff humility, 'Don't do too much, will you? Stay up for a while, but don't overdo it. You could sit on that little back verandah. It's quite a sun trap since your sister had it glassed in.'

When he goes I return to the bathroom, wash out my sweaty nightdress, and roll it in a towel. To reach the back verandah, where I mean to hang it in the sun he spoke of, I pass through the back bedroom, once my brother's room. Always a cool room, even in summer, this morning it is cold. But it is no longer a bedroom. Grace has made it into a summer sitting room. Rushmatting covers the floor, the furniture is of heavy cane, the timber walls have been stripped of paint and their good vertical grain disclosed, and traces of soil in two blue-and-white Chinese pots suggest palms or bamboo. It all looks fairly new, and attests not only to the energy of Grace's last years, but to the expansion of her interests as well. The general effect, the combined austerity and comfort, is so successful that I raise my eyebrows and blink in insulting amazement, as I used to do to annoy her when we were girls.

I open the door to the back verandah and am dazzled, first by the flood of sunlight and the cool black shine of the floor, and then by a view through the glass of a garden so fresh and verdant, so deep and rich and detailed, that I wonder for a moment if the glass is tinted. A glance at the sky assures me that it is not. I open the door and go with great care, concentrating only on my feet, down the back stairs.

Again they are fourteen planks spanning air, but narrower than in the front, and set in this case parallel to the house and propped against a little square platform. I hang my wet things on a small revolving hoist at the foot of the steps and turn to examine the garden.

The longish grass, of which several sections are of an even richer green than the rest, thins out under the big mango tree and the canopy of the persimmon. Shrubs conceal the high fences, and in the deep shade of the mango tree stands a garden seat of white iron. At the end of the garden, where for a decade after my father's death stood the gradually sagging stable and buggy shed, is an uneven hillocky area thickly overgrown with green.

Certainly, beyond the mango tree a small section of the Wilmots' house is visible, but one can always refuse to look beyond the mango tree.

Drawn to the hillocks, I am about to start down the stone path when Betty Cust, hurrying in a controlled way, comes down the back stairs.

'Nora, should you be out here?'

'I think so.'

She has arrived at the foot of the steps. She looks into my face with a hint of censure. 'Well, I hope you know best.'

She is wearing a teal-blue suit, brand new and lamentable. 'Are you going out?' I ask.

'To church.'

I try to make my face respectful, but she is looking beyond me to the mango tree.

'Gary Wilmot will ask you to cut down that tree.'

'Then he will ask in vain.'

'He used to ask Grace in vain, too.'

Standing about four feet apart, both with our hands clasped at our waists, we smile. I turn and point to the end of the garden. 'I'm taking a walk to the hilly country.'

She falls in beside me as I start down the path. 'Why is all this so green?' I ask.

'It is, isn't it? I haven't been down here for a month or so. But I think a lot of it's winter grass. A weed, you know. It will die off any day now.'

'It's not all weed.'

'No, well, this is the part Grace concentrated on. She had to let the front go, it was too big.'

'And too public. But in this drought, why has this part stayed so green? Although,' I add politely, 'I know Jack waters it.'

'Yes, and Peter has a man come in and cut the grass now and again. But I suppose the real reason it's so green is because of Grace's compost. People used to laugh at her, she was so fanatical about it. She used to say it was more than a method of gardening, it was a whole philosophy.'

'Oh, dear,' I say. I am very much on my guard. Somewhere in this, there will be one of Grace's morals, waiting to spoil the garden for me.

'She even tried to found a society,' says Betty.

'A compost society. Dear, dear, dear.'

'And got so annoyed when people weren't interested. You'll find all the books about it upstairs.'

'I don't doubt it.'

'She spread layer after layer of it here. She used to say it would resist any drought if you didn't dig it in. What a pity she didn't live to see it proved. See those very green bits? They were her vegetable beds.'

I am more on my guard than ever, almost suspecting by now a posthumous stratagem of Grace's to convert me at last to her strenuous ways. 'I am quite certain,' I say, 'that it looks much better without beds of any kind at all.'

But Betty agrees at once. 'I think so, too. It's like a little wild park, isn't it? This mound here, what you called the hilly country, this was her compost heap. It's all tumbled down now, but it was quite elaborate, with a louvred shelter and everything. Peter had the structure taken away, and he said something to Jack about having the ground levelled out.'

'Not in my lifetime.' The mound is covered with nasturtium leaves, some as big as small plates, though not one flower is visible. I bend and pick a bunch of the smaller leaves. 'I am very fond of these in a sandwich, with a little cottage cheese.'

'She did work hard here,' says Betty in rather a wistful voice.

'I can see that she did. And in those two back rooms as well.'

'They were the last things she did. She was so strong-willed.'

'Always. And so busy.'

'Yes, always.'

'I intend to make those two back rooms my quarters.'

'They were hers. She slept on that verandah.'

'What, in that glass box?'

'Winter and summer.'

'But the moonlight!'

'There are dark green blinds. Perhaps she drew them. I don't know.'

Betty now seems sad and troubled. We turn from the hillock and retrace our steps down the path. I am watching my feet, because the stone here is uneven. 'Was she happy?' I ask.

Betty, walking beside me with her arms folded, gives the question her consideration. I sit on the white iron seat under the mango tree, and in imitation of some remembered gesture, raise my bouquet of green leaves with a flourish to my nose.

'No,' replies Betty.

Beside me on the ground is a shallow earthenware dish.

Betty picks it up and goes to fill it at the nearby tap. 'No,' she says again, as she comes back and sets it down.

'Why not?'

'I don't know, Nora.'

'Did she know?'

Betty shrugs, makes a doubtful mouth. 'She once said she did.'

'What did she say?'

'That for the whole of her life, she had tried to have faith, and that for the whole of her life, she had only opinions.'

I point to the dish. Unwilling to allow that Grace has touched my heart at last, I speak curtly. 'Is that for the birds?'

'Yes. Jack fills it when he thinks of it.'

'I suppose the bird books are with the compost books.'

Betty gives a sort of giggle. 'There wasn't one she couldn't name.'

But the course of forgiveness is evidently not easy to reverse. I cannot help but think of Grace, grim and patient under the weight of her bucket of waste, walking down the garden path on her mission of salvage and temporary renewal, an object of mockery, good-natured or otherwise, by those lacking her intensity. I rise from my seat.

'This shade is too cold. I must go in and dress.'

'Did Gordon Rainbow say you could dress?'

'He didn't say I couldn't.'

We set out for the house, Betty adapting her steps to mine. 'At least she found plenty to do,' I say.

'So will you find plenty to do, Nora.'

'Shall I? Just at the moment I can't think what.'

'Your sewing. Oh, I know you can't do that fine work any more. But you're so clever and artistic, you can't give up your lovely sewing.'

But she is wrong. Although I am growing stronger every

day, and although my hands, blessed by sunshine and Doctor
Rainbow's care, are more pliant than for years, I shall never
sew again. During truces in my war with Gary Winston Mont-
gomery Wilmot (which I shall win), Lyn Wilmot, so that I may
advise her, cuts out dresses for her daughters on my kitchen
table, and the first time she did so I knew, by my revulsion at the
sound of her scissors in the cloth, that I would never sew again.

I have reduced my quarters to the kitchen, the bathroom,
and Grace's two back rooms, and unless circumstances drive
me elsewhere, none of the other rooms will be opened except
for professional inspection for pests. To guard against the sloth
of old age, I am careful to bring to my household tasks the
perseverance and discipline I once brought to my trade. Such
tasks are very soon finished, and there are no other demands
on my time.

Jack Cust has taught me how to use Grace's music apparatus,
and from her records I usually select something by Mozart.
Who was it who said even monkeys like Mozart? I read a little,
and I watch on television a documentary program on other
parts of this continent—deserts, rainforests, tropical reefs, and
mountains indented with snow—and realize with a quiet musing wonder, but with no discontent, that this shadow is all I
shall ever see of them. To familiar places in London, seen on
the same small screen, I respond with a detached interest that
begins to contain a touch of incredulity.

'*Once upon a time, a woman whose name is of no consequence passed that place ...*'

At the hours stipulated by the water board, I hose Grace's
remarkable garden, but am careful to preserve my amateur attitude towards it, and when I bury my fruit and vegetable leav-
ings instead of putting them out with the garbage, I address to
Grace this warning:

'*This is absolutely as far as I intend to go.*'

As Betty predicted, the garden has faded from that first stained-glass intensity with which it glowed to greet me, but it is still far greener than the land about it, and night confers on it another kind of richness. I sleep in Grace's glass room, and whenever I rise to draw the blinds against the moonlight, I am enthralled by the brilliance of the scene, the soft yet sharp delineation of the grass, the nasturtium leaves like floating silvery discs, and the weight and mystery of the black shadows. From my elevated look-out I see a low-flying bat cross the grass, drawing nearer and nearer its own shadow until both bat and shadow fly into the denser shadow of the mango tree. The shadow of the mango tree absorbs everything within its margin but the white iron seat, which stands glimmering all night, its arms held ready, like the ghost of a seat in a city park.

Not only bats drink from the earthenware dish under the mango tree. In the daytime I sit on the white seat and watch the birds. One little flock, brown and grey, with yellow beaks, comes so close that I am able to observe in detail the suavity and direction of their plumage. 'They are beyond compare,' I think. But in ten minutes or so, they begin to bore me.

Though I like to go in the Custs' car to the library and the supermarket, I resist their suggestions (without knowing why) of drives to 'beauty spots'. Doctor Rainbow, when he comes to see me, often sits for a while in the glass room. At first I felt we were on the verge of unusual questions, but this tension soon relaxed of its own accord, and now he simply sits, and talks of trivial things, and then gets up and goes on his way.

But one day he said, 'You should go out more.'

'Where to?'

'Isn't there anywhere you would like to go?'

To please him, I shut my eyes and pretend to think. I see cool brown water, and I open my eyes and say with surprise, 'I should like to see the river.'

'Then walk to the river. It's not far.'

That night I spread Mrs Partridge's celestial embroidery under the light, examine it for the last time, then wrap it in brown paper and secure it with adhesive tape. The next day I take my stick and set out. If Mrs Partridge cannot be disturbed, I shall leave it with her companion.

But though certain I am walking in the right direction, I get lost among all the modern houses. Why, the very conformation of the old paddocks has gone. And when at last I come to Mrs Partridge's house, I am not sure that it is indeed hers. Was it so brown, so dark, so low among bamboos? And where is the river that ran behind it? Beyond this house there are only roofs. When I knock, some creature, bird or lizard, bursts startlingly through the bamboo, then the resonance of my knock sinks into silence.

Still, I will walk by the river.

But nor can I find the river. And from whom can I ask directions? Two women, standing with folded arms talking on a driveway, go into the house just as I am about to hail them. And everyone else is in cars. These cars, so continuously and swiftly passing, change me from a walker to a pedestrian. I am the only pedestrian in all these streets.

I turn back the way I came, and as I make my way past fences and fancy letter-boxes, carports and garages, paved terraces and blue swimming pools, I must frequently swerve to avoid the huge dusty leaves, from monsteras and umbrella trees and the like, that hang over footpaths. How relieved I am to turn a corner and see, at the end of the next block, 'the big white corner house with the poinciana trees'.

'Gordon Rainbow should have told you,' says Betty Cust, 'that nowadays the river is accessible only in a few places.'

'Houses all along,' says Jack. 'Waterfrontages. Cost a fortune.'

The house I thought was Mrs Partridge's had belonged to

somebody else, but had been bought by developers and was about to be demolished. Shaking my head in bafflement, I laugh, and proffer the wrapped embroidery to Betty Cust.

'Please, *you* return it.'

They bring a tray of tea to the verandah, and as we drink it I describe in exaggerated terms the blows dealt to me by the monsteras.

'In my day,' I say, 'plants in these parts were not so tropical.'

'Everybody grows those things now,' says Jack. 'We grow them ourselves.'

And indeed, at the other end of the verandah, I can see the dark leaves climbing one behind the other, casting on the timber a shadow perforated by tear-shaped fragments of sunlight.

'Only natural,' says Jack. 'And eucalyptus, too. And tea-trees. Everybody grows them now.'

'Remember the things the old people grew,' says Betty.

'Mum's flowers,' says Jack. 'Larkspurs, hollyhocks.'

'Candytuft,' muses Betty, 'columbines, pinks . . .'

'I reckon the old people fought the place,' says Jack. 'They fought it.'

Well, it is too late now for me to learn not to fight it. The short walk home seems long and dusty. I see myself, as if from above, walking headlong and wildly plying my stick. It is with strong feelings of relief and finality that I reach my own domain. Goodbye, woman who used to walk, girl who used to walk. I shut another door.

The period of waiting I have now entered on resembles the first of all because once again I am waiting without panic, and with leisure at my disposal. I have had a letter from Olive. She is coming home soon to see her mother, and her mother's companion having told her that I am here, she proposes also to see me. '*That is,*' she writes, '*if you wish me to.*' I take down her last novel and look at her photograph on the back of the jacket.

How fine she looks, how stately and authoritative. No doubt I shall still annoy her. '*Yes, do come,*' I reply. '*We shall sit and quarrel under my mango tree.*'

I write a weekly letter to Hilda and Liza, and receive their replies with pleasure, but it is useless to deny that an awareness of permanent severance keeps our letters in a low key, and imbues them slightly with tiredness. They, at least, have each kept one of their former audience of three, and poor Fred, wherever he is, no doubt finds hearers for his tales of persecution. I find myself thinking that we were all great story-tellers at number six. Yes, all of us, meeting in passages or assembling in each other's quarters or in the square, were busily collating, and presenting to ourselves and the other three, the truthful fictions of our lives.

I am often lonely for that audience, and yet, if it were possible to return and regain it, I would not go. An audience, especially so sympathetic an audience, imposes restrictions I now wish to do without.

'What do you do with yourself all day long?' asks Lyn Wilmot, as I show her how to set in a sleeve.

'If you can do that,' she says, showing an inclination to prod me in the arm, 'couldn't you make something?'

But I have made things, concocted things, all my life. Perhaps I shall do so again (and indeed there are times when I do prefigure some small hand-made object), but at present my concern is to find things. My globe of memory is in free spin, with no obscure side, and although at times in its swelling and spinning it offers the queer suggestion that imagination is only memory at one, or two, or twenty, removes, my interest now is in repudiating, or in trying to repudiate, those removes, even if it ends by my finding something only as small as a stone lying on pale grass.

I believe I have found the river—the real river I disregarded on my first walks and failed to find on my last—because never before have I seen its scoured-out creeks nor known that the shadows of its brown water are lavender at evening. And one day, rising on stairs, fourteen broad planks, I see from above the two discs of a straw boater, a man's shoulders, trousered legs. Coming closer, knees rising, left-right, left-right. At arms's length now, hat tilts back, face is raised, arms fly out, gather me in. And out of that flurry, a child's shriek, rising.

'Hold me tight!'

But still, his face is as static as the face in his photograph.

I am almost angry that there continues to flash on my memory that old chimera, the step of a horse, the nod of a plume, and that always, always, it is accompanied for a second by a choking chaos of grief. But one evening, when I have sat too long under the mango tree, and I turn my head and see the first whiff of darkness extend along the grass and deepen the pockets of foliage, I remember a black cloth. A black dress, dropped over my head from above. It passes over my aching eyes, my swollen mouth, and is arranged on my shoulders by someone whose waist is at a level with my eyes. I stare at the buckle of her belt, mother-of-pearl, until it dissolves in wetness and flashes with long stars, pink and sea-green stars. The same wetness diffuses the darkening grass of Grace's garden, and then out of a moment of groping, of intense confusion, comes the step of a horse, the nod of a plume, come the plumed heads of the curbed horses at my father's funeral.

Later, I remember that there was a voice, too, with rolling r's.

'A fine ceremony, madam! A verrry fine ceremony!'

I think it consoled me, a little. I think ceremony always has, a little.

AFTERWORD

'WHO DO YOU THINK YOU ARE?'
BY ANNA FUNDER

First, a confession. I am not coming to this novel fresh, as an adult reader with a hard-won but mostly stable sense of self from which to survey the world, written and real. I read *Tirra Lirra by the River* at school thirty years ago. It entered my blood in such a way that I cannot remember a 'self' before this book was part of it.

From the vantage point of my now forty-seven years, it seems to me that the ages between, say, thirteen and twenty-three are particularly dangerous in a duckling kind of way for the retaining of impressions, the unknown setting of patterns, that are then, apparently instinctively, followed. We form our tastes, especially literary and sexual, by what we come across—or what comes across us—in those years.

And, though this dangerous decade can seem like a time of unbounded possibility—most of life, after all, being still to come—these are also years in which some of the imprinting sets limits to our sense of what is possible.

Tirra Lirra by the River is a novel that examines in brutally, beautifully honest detail the patterns etched on a soul at this formative time. And it shows how, late in life—however well, or less well, you might think that has turned out—there may be some satisfaction to be had by recognizing these patterns, and what they have made of us. Nora Porteous is an old woman who has come home and she is looking for what it was that made her, and trying to account for what she then made of herself. These are confronting questions to unravel, and ones that the novel, in some small way, also poses for me now.

In the mid-1980s, *Tirra Lirra by the River* was a set text for secondary school students in Melbourne, Australia, along with Christina Stead's masterpiece *The Man Who Loved Children*, and Carson McCullers's sublime *The Member of the Wedding*. These books have stayed with me in a way so deep that I cannot unravel them from the writer, or the woman, I have become.

All three books are about extraordinary teenage misfits: the genius Louie and the 'freak' Frankie—who inhabit the extraordinary writers Stead and McCullers—and Jessica Anderson's Nora, wry and brave. When I reread them now, I see that they are a trifecta of high art and terror and truth almost too powerful to give to teenagers, which is to say exactly what they crave and need (as opposed to 'relevant' books about 'issues' which are 'resolved' in candy-floss epiphanies and 'growth and change moments').

Still, a small part of me—perhaps the part that is now mother to preteen girls—does wonder if this stunning, toxic cocktail that formed me was not too strong. Did it feed a monster? Comfort or encourage something that should have been put in a sack and sunk? Who knows: life, especially a single life, is both the control and the experiment. What did they think would happen to us, back in a suburban girls' school in the lost, pre-grunge, hair-gelled 1980s?

I've no idea what I would have been like without these books. Except more lost.

But why did this novel mean so much? After all, it was about the struggles of a woman to live a life in which she can create works of art, fully seventy years earlier. Hadn't the world changed radically for the better by the time it was published in 1978? We'd had another wave of feminism in the Western world, and, in Australia, the extraordinary Whitlam Labor government's social reforms: universal free health care, free university education, no-fault divorce, the single mother's pension, the establishment of the Australia Council for the Arts and the Human Rights and Equal Opportunity Commission, antidiscrimination laws, multicultural policy and so on. As a teenager I blithely considered myself a beneficiary of this new, just, well-funded world. I could get sick, educated, divorced, raise my children alone and have all my future novels (in which I could out myself without recrimination as whatever I liked) funded on the public purse. But no amount of teen dreaming or government subsidy can resolve the questions of how to find a form of life that suits you, and how to be an artist. These questions of sex and art are at the heart of *Tirra Lirra by the River*.

'When my worst expectations are met,' Nora confides in the first pages, 'I frequently find alleviation in detaching myself from the action, as it were, the better to appreciate ... the pattern of doom, or comedy, or whatever you like to call it.'

What if we liked to call 'the pattern of doom, or comedy, or whatever' a novel—indeed this novel? *Tirra Lirra by the River* is an intricate tissue of reminiscence woven by an old woman as she examines her life, pulling threads through it and tying loose ends to their long-ago beginnings. Because Nora is someone compelled to make things—beautiful, useless things, but things the making of which is absolutely necessary to her—her struggles are the struggles of an artist. There are two of them. First, to find some form of life which allows her to work *and* to have a personal, sexual life (not easy for anyone, especially a woman, and most especially a woman of Nora's time and place). And then there's the struggle involved in the act of making art—of imposing form on her material, finding 'the pattern of doom, or comedy, or whatever' in it.

Looked at this way, Anderson's novel is an enactment of what it is about, as, more obviously, Ian McEwan's novel *Atonement* is itself the act of atonement for its narrator. Or, perhaps, in the self-referentially startling way that an Escher drawing is a drawing of the hand that made the drawing, in the act of making it. We are in the narrator Nora's mind as she makes her work, and we discern, or imagine we do, the Escher-like hand of Jessica Anderson enacting her own much more successful struggle, and producing this book.

I was fortunate to be able to speak with Anderson's daughter, the eminent screenwriter Laura Jones (*Oscar and Lucinda*, *The Portrait of a Lady*, *An Angel at My Table*). Jones told me her mother's belief was that truly terrible subjects become bearable to us in art, because the art itself—the beauty of form—offers a kind of consolation. Form is the pattern imposed on material or, as the critic Kenneth Burke had it, 'the satisfaction of an expectation.'

The satisfactions—or consolations—of art in *Tirra Lirra by the River* are profound. Possibly they are so profound that they can distract us from the story itself, a story which, on one reading at least, is a tragedy of 'vile wastage, vile wastage': the waste of an artist's talent.

When I was searching for how to think of this novel, what came to mind was something small and made of material denser than we usually find—like a rock of previously unknown qualities from another planet. Or perhaps a Leonardo painting, in which behind the mysteriously smiling girl there is a landscape with a castle, in the window of which is an artist painting a smiling girl in a landscape with a castle behind her, in the window of which . . . and so on. There is so much surreptitiously packed into these pages. And yet, on its surface, this novel achieves the apparent simplicity its narrator recognizes as the hard-won achievement of a great artist.

Anderson was in her early sixties when *Tirra Lirra by the River* was published. It was rapturously received in Australia, and won the nation's most prestigious prize for fiction, the Miles Franklin. Readers loved it, no doubt responding to all kinds of truths in it, to the point where they assumed events it described to be literally true. Laura Jones told me that, when interviewed, her mother would insist that the book could not be autobiographical, since 'Nora was born at the turn of the century. [*Pause.*] I was born in 1916 ...' 'As if,' Jones said with a smile, 'that settled it.'

When readers assume the literal truth of fiction, it can give a writer a double-edged feeling. In a way, it's a compliment: they have found this art to ring true. At the same time, to assume a one-to-one correspondence to the writer's life is to doubt the artist's powers to invent. Worse, it is to imagine an open window, even an invitation, to climb in and rummage through the writer's private life, looking for evidence to tie them to their fictions. Jones says her mother reacted testily, as well one might, to the assumption of literal parallels with Nora. 'See?' Anderson would say, lifting her hair back off her face. 'No scars. No facelift.' With one startling gesture she defended both her private self and the primacy of her imagination.

The book begins in the late 1970s, with Nora coming back to Brisbane. Her life, in one view, has been a series of escapes from constraints on full personhood for a woman: most notably from Australia, and from marriage. As a young woman she escaped Brisbane's 'rawness and weak gentility, its innocence and deep deceptions' for marriage and Sydney. Then she escaped the latter for some forty years in London. Nora has come back only because she has run out of options.

Now she is old. As she enters her childhood home, left to her after the death of her sister Grace, she sees 'a shape pass' in the hallway mirror. 'It is the shape of an old woman who began to call herself old before she really was, partly to get in first and partly out of a fastidiousness about the word "elderly", but who is now really old. She has allowed her shoulders to slump. I press back my shoulders and make first for the living room.'

From the first pages, it is clear that we are in the hands, or the mind, of someone of great, humorous self-consciousness, who can see herself from almost every angle, 360 degrees around: 'I' and 'she' at close quarters.

Nora enters the living room, a room of which she has strange expectations—of exaltation, mysterious bliss—that she fully expects to be dashed. 'Things are turning out so badly,' she thinks, 'that I am filled again with my perverse contentment.' This 'perverse contentment' I recognize in a deep way from home, from early imprinting of my own. I associate it, possibly irrationally, with the Irish-Australian heritage that Anderson and I, in part, share. It is the foretelling of misfortune as the underdog's pale triumph. At least, the thinking goes, if the worst does come to pass, you'll have the grim satisfaction of having been right: the universe might disappoint you, but it could not prove you wrong. I associate it with my mother and her downtrodden forebears; a mind-set bent on pulling wry, self-righteous satisfaction from oppression or mishap. (It works, in my observation, until the end really *is* nigh, when the fact that you predicted it turns out to be no consolation at all.)

But Nora is looking for something important, something close to the beginning of it all—and she finds it. It is the picture

made by the distortion in the 'cheap thick glass,' in the living
room window, 'a miniature landscape of mountains and valleys
with a tiny castle, weird and ruined, set on one slope.' In her
childhood she had been 'deeply engrossed by those miniature
landscapes, green, wet, romantic, with silver serpentine rivulets, and flashing lakes, and castles moulded out of any old stick
or stone. I believe they enchanted me.' Later, in her teen years,
when she reads *The Lady of Shalott*, she discovers that her fan-
tasy place already had a name: Camelot.

> I no longer looked through the glass. I no longer needed
> to. In fact, to do so would have broken rather than sus-
> tained the spell, because that landscape had become a re-
> gion of my mind, where infinite expansion was possible,
> and where no obtrusion, such as the discomfort of knees
> imprinted by the cane of a chair, or a magpie alighting
> on the grass and shattering the miniature scale, could
> prevent the emergence of Sir Lancelot.

And then he comes:

> From underneath his helmet flowed
> His coal-black curls as on he rode,
>   As he rode down to Camelot.
> From the bank and from the river
> He flashed into the crystal mirror,
> 'Tirra lirra,' by the river
>   Sang Sir Lancelot.

> The book was one of my father's.

Tennyson's poem is a romance in which longing for a man
causes a woman artist to abandon her work, which brings down

a curse upon her and she dies. When we meet her, the Lady sits in her tower. Like Nora, she makes weavings, and like Nora, she is under some kind of spell that keeps her apart from life. Though she 'knows not what the curse may be,' the Lady must stay put, looking only in the mirror 'that hangs before her all the year' in which the 'shadows of the world appear'. So she sits out her life, making her work. The Lady must not break the spell by leaving her tower to try to get to Camelot.

But isolation, even if it is necessary for artistic work, cannot be sustained against the longing for love and the real world.

> Came two young lovers lately wed;
> 'I am half sick of shadows,' said
>   The Lady of Shalott.

If the verse Nora remembers reflects her desire for Lancelot—as lover, or father—it is the next verse of Tennyson's poem, not in the novel, which seems to encompass its action:

> She left the web, she left the loom,
> She made three paces thro' the room,
> She saw the water-lily bloom,
> She saw the helmet and the plume,
>   She look'd down to Camelot.
> Out flew the web and floated wide;
> The mirror crack'd from side to side;
> 'The curse is come upon me!' cried
>   The Lady of Shalott.

The Lady is cursed when she dares go after life and love. She gets in a boat and quietly expires, floating down to Camelot. The curse is twofold. It is the specific curse of the artist, who must remain apart from the world in order to represent it. And

it is the general one, hoary and old and unfathomable as patri-
archy, in which a woman passively submits to parameters she
cannot choose, and so a tragedy—operatic or poetic or novelis-
tic—can be made of her exquisite, fated succumbing. (If it were
Lancelot who left the tower, lay down in a boat and died, there
would be no poem, because there would simply be no action.
For some—again hoary and old and unfathomable—reason, as
we know, large tracts of Western art are founded on women's
fantasized tragic passivity.)

Nora is cursed with wanting life and art—desires that in Brisbane in the early twentieth century could not speak their name,
and that are probably pretty difficult to reconcile, without a lot
of collateral damage, in any life. Indeed as I write this, in time
bought from a babysitter, bargained from my husband and stolen from my children, the risk of collateral damage feels closer
than I'd like. And yet, though I have read my Anderson and my
Tennyson and know the risks, what I find myself most wanting—
at least from time to time—is a nice, high tower all of my own.

As a girl, Nora inhabits a world of women who are either chaf-
ing at or enforcing the limits of that world. Nora's father died
when she was six, and she lives with her sister and her mother,
who, as she says with admirable, now anachronistic lack of self-
pity, 'didn't like me much.' ('Our natures were antipathetic. It
happens more often than is admitted.') A brother dies in World
War I. Nora suffers from the longing to be elsewhere, some-
where she imagines real life is possible.

Nora's foils—those examples of alternative fates—are two
other young women. Olive Partridge is a literary girl. She will
have three hundred pounds a year when she turns twenty-five,
and, as she says, 'that very minute I'm off.' Dorothy Irey is beautiful and quiet and seems too aesthetic for this place. As she and

Nora cross paths on their obsessive, frustrated, 'lonely walking' of the streets and paths of Brisbane, Nora notices Dorothy's fingers 'nibbling together.' At home, Nora wonders to her sister, 'Why does Dorothy Irey stay here?' But Grace turns on her 'in a fury' saying, 'We don't all think we're too good for this place, Lady Muck.' Like Nora's mother and, later, her hideous mother-in-law, Una Porteous, Grace is a self-appointed policewoman of other women's legitimate desires.

While she waits for her life to take shape, Nora makes embroidered wall hangings with her energies and time. Dorothy Irey gets married and stops walking. She is busy, Nora presumes, with a house and babies.

> Grace answered my enquiries by saying with the old anger that of course she was happy.
> 'Why wouldn't she be? She has all any reasonable person could want.'

The question of what one might reasonably want, the tailoring of desire to social limits, runs through the book as it runs through all our lives. And those limits are policed with a question: 'Who does she think *she* is?' This is a question of multipurpose violence, which can be applied with equal ease to shrivel artistic ambition as well as sexual desire. This question is, one might say, how the curse of female passivity is kept alive. It is how the tower is patrolled.

This is how it works with sex. When Nora is in her teens, a group of boys—polite when alone, rapacious as a group—try to grope the girls, who are varying degrees of willing.

> If they could entice or trick one of us away from the others, they would grab us and throw us to the ground. They would try to pull down our pants one minute and

abjectly beg the next. As we made our escape they would villify us horribly.

Nobody was raped. Escape was optional, and for me, in spite of my sexual excitement, imperative. I hated being pulled about and roughly handled. It made me bored and grieved and angry.

'What did you come for then?'

I saw sense in the question, and stopped going. Those girls who continued to go began to treat me with enmity, and for the first time I took note of an ominous growled-out question.

'Who does *she* think she is?'

I'm disturbed by the extent to which Nora's girlhood seventy years earlier resonated with us as we grew up in 1980s Australia. We are led to believe that sex had been 'liberated' fully a generation earlier in the 1960s, but like all regime change, the results of the sexual revolution were more uneven than advertised. In the 1930s, Nora's husband at first calls her 'frigid' and then, when she starts to get pleasure from sex, a 'whore'. I remember similar kinds of sexual shunning applied to girls, when the slippery slope from 'frigid' to 'cocktease' to 'slut' was vertiginous and absolute, and you could be shunted from one category to another without, for your trouble, having had any fun at all. And I remember the policing question, too, muttered most often by other girls, not directly to you but deliberately within your hearing: 'Who does she think *she* is?' In fact, the question was so brutal and basic that it could be asked without any words at all, just by a look.

At Olive Partridge's going-away party, Nora stumbles upon her Lancelot. He is a dark, thin man, not young, 'the look in his eyes like a caught breath.' She runs into a room to catch her own breath. When she comes back to find him, he's gone, replaced by a pale imitation, his nephew, Colin Porteous.

'I knew it was him you came back to find,' said Colin Porteous. 'I could tell by the way you looked at him.'

'How do you know how I looked at him?' I asked furiously.

'Because I was standing here beside him.'

The man she wanted is gone. 'I couldn't speak. [Colin] came a step nearer and looked closely into my face. "Well, well, well. My, oh, my."' The stand-in is able to humiliate her, simply because he witnessed her desire.

Nevertheless, Nora marries this substitute Lancelot, and so makes her escape to Sydney, which, with 'what little common sense I had,' had become a stand-in for Camelot. The couple lives in a flat in Bomera, a dilapidated mansion right on Sydney Harbour at Potts Point (still gloriously there, and worth a Google). And it is at Bomera where, for the first time, Nora makes friends with other artists. As the horror of her marriage unfolds, she realizes she is more comfortable in their company than her husband's. They are people who understand implicitly the need to make something, to create. 'All I wanted in the world was to be left alone in my beautiful room, close to people who never asked, audibly or otherwise, who I thought *I* was, but who nevertheless were interested in the answer to that question.'

When the Depression comes, the couple leaves the beauty of the harbour and moves in with Colin's mother, Una, into a 'big flat chequerboard suburb, predominately iron-grey.' Whether they really need to move for financial reasons or whether Colin just wants to be closer to his grotesque and doting mother is not clear. Nora's entrapment and misery out there is profound and lasts for years. It is the shocking poverty and dependence of a wife who must steal pennies from her husband's or mother-in-law's purse, taking care not to let the coins chink, and whose yearning for freedom is reduced, once again, to desperate walking. Strangely, these were the things—utterly beyond my experience in every way—that stuck fastest to the teenage flypaper mind. Why?

We read Henry James or Edith Wharton or Tolstoy not because the social conditions and mores are the same, but because the human condition of ducking and weaving around them, of conformity and rebellion—and their price—are. What is the price to be paid for straining at the socially acceptable edges of happiness? A novel—this novel—might show you.

When I was a teenager, powerless myself and trapped in a maze of strict expectations, spoken and unspoken, it was Nora's entrapment I noticed most. But now what shocks me more is the corrosive effect of her passivity and the way, as she says, that '[m]uch of my long life can be apportioned into periods of waiting' to escape. This passivity, combined with the persistent underestimating of her own talents, concocts a trope so perniciously feminine that to write of it even now feels like invoking a curse.

Nora's marriage ends, and she goes to London. On the ship she has an affair with a genial, married American which reveals to her a reality of love, that 'far surpassed the theory.' She recalls, 'At last, I thought, I knew how freedom could be reconciled with appeasement.' But she ends that relationship at the dock. In London, she discovers she is pregnant and suffers a horrific abortion. Afterward, Nora decides to end her sex life.

Which leaves the artistic life as the one remaining to her. But whether she is consciously aware of being an artist is a major question of the novel.

Anderson described Nora to an interviewer as a woman 'who was actually a born artist, but was in a place where artists, although they were known to exist, were supposed to exist elsewhere. She was born among that kind of people, and she herself doesn't know that she's an artist. She struggles through, trying to arrive at her art and never succeeding.'

When asked if the backbone of the novel were, to her, 'the plight of the unrecognized artist,' Anderson described a plight more fundamental:

> Not an unrecognized artist, but a person who *is* an artist but doesn't succeed even in being *conscious* of being an artist. She had a kind of buried talent, buried in herself. The sewing, the tapestries, had to be something acceptable to her society. She wasn't a strongly original person. Not many of us are.

To be a strongly original person takes acres of secret confidence, endogenous or achieved. The vicious, kneecapping question 'Who do you think you are?' seems to have entered Nora's consciousness so early and so profoundly that it was simply not possible for her to imagine herself as an artist.

How much of this is to do with being a woman of her time, place and economic circumstance and how much (if any) is particularly Australian is hard to tell. Certainly, artists and intellectuals of Nora's generation, such as Christina Stead, felt they had to leave Australia, as would the generation after hers (among them Germaine Greer, Clive James, Robert Hughes, Michael Blakemore and Jeffrey Smart). I sometimes think that the justly vaunted egalitarianism of Australia, the 'fair go' which had its apotheosis in the Whitlam 1970s of my childhood, had a darker flip side. Just as the fairness of Australian society goes back over a century in no small measure to an Irish Catholic tradition of social justice which set limits on (often English) power, I imagine, too, that the Irish Catholic underdog thinking came with it, as its shadow. Possibly this is best explained in an old (and not very funny) joke: An American, an Englishman and an Australian are digging a ditch. The boss drives past in a Rolls-Royce. The Englishman: 'Lovely car, but personally I would always choose the Bentley over the Rolls.' The American: 'One day, folks, that's gonna be me riding up there.' The Australian: 'One day that bastard's going to be back down here in this ditch with the rest of us where he belongs.' Or, put another way, 'Who does he think he is?'

But escape is possible. Nora's friend Olive Partridge, who has money, gets to London where she can express her artistic ambition. Olive says, 'I want to be simple, utterly simple. Like water.' Nora tells her, 'No chance. You'll never be simple, and neither shall I. We had to start disguising ourselves too early.' Olive is then struck by Nora's intelligence, which Nora laughs off, in that modest way in which women do, thereby damaging themselves. But old Nora acknowledges, 'Of course, I underestimated Olive. If she did not arrive at simplicity in her person, she did so in her later books, whereas I never have, in anything.' A judgement she must later, fortunately, modify.

If you are a born artist, can you survive if you cannot make anything? The making of things is necessary for artists of any medium to find their way to be in the world. If Nora is not making something, she is not really alive, much as a writer who is not writing is miserable. If you step outside your tower and stop work, you feel dead.

Or you feel like killing someone. Nora's childhood friend and fellow walker Dorothy Rainbow, née Irey, is a creative soul trapped in a life of marriage and babies. Dorothy meets an end of almost unspeakable violence and tragedy. (One of the most moving things in the novel is the magnificent restraint of Nora's interactions with Gordon Rainbow, Dorothy's only surviving child.) At a very low point of her own, Nora remembers her old acquaintance: 'I ask myself why Dorothy Rainbow did not hang on, provisionally, and why nothing was offered to appease the remnants of that need that once drove her to walk.'

But Nora must know why. Dorothy, trapped in Brisbane within the confines of what she could 'reasonably want,' had no chance. Whereas Nora, in London, had found solace among a second community of creative people, making costumes for the theatre. 'Before a week was out,' she remembers, 'it was clear that I had fallen among people who would accept me for what I was, whatever I was.' Even though being among them has saved her life, the curse of '*Who do you think you are?*' is so strong that Nora persists in not daring to name herself as an artist of any kind.

And yet, when the older Nora is presented on three separate occasions with embroideries she made all those years ago, her tone changes radically. Gone is the diffident underdog. In its stead is the confident voice of an artist with a gimlet eye, critically evaluating her work. Each time she examines one of the works, the tone shift is so radical that the fabric of the novel seems to tear a little, revealing, Escher-like, the hand of the artist behind it.

When shown the first embroidery, Nora is 'so astonished by the excellence of the design and the beauty of the colour' she cannot speak. It is of an orange tree with eight little birds, 'all fabulous yet touchingly domestic' which 'strut or peck beneath it.' She declares to herself, 'They are in danger of giving it a spotty effect, and yet they don't, and that risk, taken and surmounted, is its merit and distinction.' The second embroidery is of a magpie thrusting its head through the leaves of a

jacaranda tree. It is a disappointment so Nora immediately suspects the brilliant orange tree was a fluke. Her carer, Betty Cust,
offers words of comfort: 'You would think that maggie was real.'
Nora's next thought gets a paragraph of its own:

> 'The criteria of even the most trivial art are not those
> of virtue.'

When Betty brings in the third work, a design of swirling
suns, moon and stars, Nora is floored by it. Its excellence 'disturbs as well as amazes' her and prompts her to ask aloud in
Betty's presence what she was running from all those years.

> 'I wonder what would have happened if I had never left
> this place.'
>   'Haven't you ever wondered before?'
>   'Never. Never once. I always believed it was impera-
> tive. But this shows I had begun to do something here
> after all. I have never done anything of this quality since.
> Who knows what else I may have drawn ...'
>   I stop myself in time. The words in my mind were
> 'drawn out of the compression of a secret life'.

The possibility of regret for an artistic life unlived is unspoken
and terrible. It is so hard for any artist to know how much they
need the constraints of their tower, and how much they need
the freedom—at the risk of lostness, or lost focus—outside it.
But at the same time this is Nora's victory: she sees that she
made something out of what looked like nothing, like entrapment, like waiting. Though, in typical fashion, hers is a silent
victory. Nora cannot utter the words even to kind, perceptive
Betty Cust, because to do so would be to admit to having had
an ambition, like the Lady of Shalott's, to be both in the world

and in the artist's tower, using the world as material. Then, as now, this is to court psychological and financial danger, and it may also still be to bring a curse down on your head. Whether you are cursed or not will probably depend on what you find yourself able, in your own time and place, to draw out of 'the compression of a secret life.'

I didn't consciously think about this book for thirty years. But, as Nora says, 'I did not know that such infections can enter the blood, and that a tertiary stage is possible'. I wrote a novel with a wry old narrator who deals with her Australian carer in the present tense, while reexamining and reassembling the puzzle of her past. There are words, scenes and a whole tone of caustic hope-hedging that I can see now are shocking echoes of the pattern this novel imprinted on me.

Which leaves me experiencing an impulse like an alcoholic at AA who must go back through all their acquaintances, hunt them down on Facebook or in life and apologize for what they did when they were drinking, even if they can't remember what it was. Is it even possible to go back through all your reading and acknowledge what you took, though you didn't know you took it? If I am honest, I should add that I have also secretly long considered myself at the same time a skinny misfit Frankie Addams, fallen off the known world, and a great fat lugubrious Louie Pollitt, plotting her escape from it.

My old-woman narrator, Ruth, possibly puts it better than I can: 'Some memories may not even be my own. I heard the stories so often I took them into me, burnished and smothered them as an oyster a piece of grit, and now, mine or not, they are my shiniest self.'

The oyster no more chooses the grit that gets into its shell than we choose which books get under our skin. Nor, I suppose, can I be any more accountable than a bicuspid for the shape and colour of what I might, years later, cough up. And it is in this way, in the end, that I feel that though I did not steal anything and I cannot give it back, what I can do is acknowledge, in gratitude and awe, what I owe. Or, as Nora puts it, 'Imagination is only memory at one, or two, or twenty, removes'—and to know that is to repudiate those moves.

THE NEVERSINK LIBRARY

THE NEVERSINK LIBRARY

THE TRAVELS AND SURPRISING ADVENTURES OF BARON MUNCHAUSEN
by Rudolf Erich Raspe

978-1-61219-123-2
$16.00 / $16.00 CAN

SNOWBALL'S CHANCE
by John Reed

978-1-61219-125-6
$15.00 / $15.00 CAN

FUTILITY
by William Gerhardie

978-1-61219-145-4
$15.00 / $15.00 CAN

THE REVERBERATOR
by Henry James

978-1-61219-156-0
$15.00 / $15.00 CAN

THE RIGHT WAY TO DO WRONG
by Harry Houdini

978-1-61219-166-9
$15.00 / $15.00 CAN

A COUNTRY DOCTOR'S NOTEBOOK
by Mikhail Bulgakov

978-1-61219-190-4
$15.00 / $15.00 CAN

I AWAIT THE DEVIL'S COMING
by Mary MacLane

978-1-61219-194-2
$16.00 / $16.00 CAN

THE POLYGLOTS
by William Gerhardie

978-1-61219-188-1
$17.00 / $17.00 CAN

MY AUTOBIOGRAPHY
by Charlie Chaplin

978-1-61219-192-8
$20.00 / $20.00 CAN

WHERE THERE'S LOVE, THERE'S HATE
by Adolfo Bioy Casares
and Silvina Ocampo

978-1-61219-150-8
$15.00 / $15.00 CAN

THE DIFFICULTY OF BEING
by Jean Cocteau

978-1-61219-290-1
$15.95 / $15.95 CAN

THE NEVERSINK LIBRARY